THE PERFECT PEARL

Norita Combe, finding herself penniless after her father's death, goes to seek the help of her old Governess who is looking after the daughter of the Marquis of Hawkhurst.

She finds on arrival at his house in London that her Governess has to leave immediately because her sister is ill.

Norita takes her place, the Governess being sure that she will see very little of the Marquis, who is engaged in a passionate love-affair with a great Beauty, Lady Bettine Daviot.

Lady Bettine, however, demands pearls from the Marquis and, on an impulse, he thinks it would be amusing to take a party to Bahrain to see the divers collecting the oysters in the Persian Gulf.

How within twenty-four hours Norita finds herself swept away with Alyce, the child she is looking after on the Marquis's yacht; how when she encounters the Marquis she finds him very different from what she expected; and how in Bahrain the traditional pirates constitute a danger from which only the Marquis can save her and Alyce, is told in this exciting and unusual story – the 416th book by Barbara Cartland.

**Also by the same author,
and available from NEL:**

NEVER FORGET LOVE
THERESA AND A TIGER
THE PERFUME OF THE GODS

THE PERFECT PEARL

Barbara Cartland

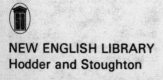

NEW ENGLISH LIBRARY
Hodder and Stoughton

Copyright ©1988 by
Barbara Cartland

First published in Great
Britain in 1989
by New English Library
Paperbacks

A New English Library
Paperback Original

Printed and bound in Great
Britain for Hodder and Stoughton
Paperbacks, a division of Hodder
and Stoughton Ltd., Mill Road,
Dunton Green, Sevenoaks, Kent
TN13 2YA (Editorial Office: 47
Bedford Square, London, WC1B
3DP) by Cox & Wyman Ltd.,
Reading, Berks.

British Library C.I.P.

Cartland, Barbara, *1902–*
  The perfect pearl.
  I. Title
  823'.912[F]

ISBN 0-450-49180-3

ABOUT THE AUTHOR

BARBARA CARTLAND, the world's most famous romantic novelist, who is also an historian, playwright, lecturer, political speaker and television personality, has now written over 470 books and sold nearly 500 million all over the world.

She has also had many historical works published and has written four autobiographies as well as the biographies of her mother and that of her brother, Ronald Cartland, who was the first Member of Parliament to be killed in the last war. This book has a preface by Sir Winston Churchill and has just been republished with an introduction by Sir Arthur Bryant.

"Love at the Helm", a novel written with the help and inspiration of the late Earl Mountbatten of Burma, Great Uncle of His Royal Highness The Prince of Wales, is being sold for the Mountbatten Memorial Trust.

Miss Cartland in 1978 sang an *Album of Love Songs* with the Royal Philharmonic Orchestra.

In 1976, by writing 21 books, she broke the world record and has continued for the following ten years with 24, 20, 23, 24, 25, 22, 26, 24 and 23. In the *Guinness Book of Records* she is listed as the world's top-selling author.

In private life Barbara Cartland, who is a Dame of Grace of the Order of St. John of Jerusalem, Chairman of the St. John Council in Hertfordshire and Deputy President of the St. John Ambulance Brigade, has fought for better conditions and salaries for Midwives and Nurses.

She has championed the cause for old people, had the Law altered regarding gypsies and founded the first Romany Gypsy Camp in the world.

Her designs, "Decorating with Love", are being sold all over the U.S.A. and the National Home Fashions League made her, in 1981, "Woman of Achievement".

Barbara Cartland's Book, 'Getting Older, Growing Younger", and her cookery book, "The Romance of Food", have been published in Great Britain, the U.S.A. and in other parts of the world.

She has also written a Children's Pop-Up book entitled "Princess to the Rescue".

In 1984 she received, at Kennedy Airport, America's Bishop Wright Air Industry Award for her contribution to the development of aviation when in 1931, she and two R.A.F. Officers thought of, and carried, the first aeroplane-towed glider air-mail. In January 1988 she went to the Mairie de Paris to receive La Médaille de la Ville de Paris (the Gold Medal of the City of Paris).

An experiment took place last year with Barbara Cartland which had never happened with any author before.

Eagle Moss (Patrick Cavendish) brought out a hardback book every fortnight at £1.95. Beautifully bound in red and gold leather it made a Barbara Cartland Library.

In 1964 she founded the National Association for Health and is now the President, as a front for all the Health Stores and any product made as alternative medicine.

This has now a £500,000,000 turnover a year, with one third going in export.

OTHER BOOKS BY
BARBARA CARTLAND

Romantic Novels, over 400, the most recently published being:

Love and Kisses
Sapphires in Siam
A Caretaker of Love
Secrets of the Heart
Riding in the Sky
Lovers in Lisbon
Love is Invincible
The Goddess of Love
An Adventure of Love
The Herb for Happiness

Only a Dream
Saved By Love
Little Tongues of Fire
A Chieftain Finds Love
The Lovely Liar
The Perfume of the Gods
A Knight in Paris
Revenge is Sweet
The Passionate Princess
Solita and the Spies

The Dream and the Glory
(In aid of the St. John Ambulance Brigade)

Autobiographical and Biographical:

The Isthmus Years 1919–1939
The Years of Opportunity 1939–1945
I Search for Rainbows 1945–1976
We Danced All Night 1919–1929
Ronald Cartland (With a foreword by Sir Winston Churchill)
Polly – My Wonderful Mother
I Seek the Miraculous

Historical:

Bewitching Women
The Outrageous Queen (The Story of Queen Christina of Sweden)
The Scandalous Life of King Carol
The Private Life of Charles II
The Private Life of Elizabeth, Empress of Austria
Josephine, Empress of France
Diana de Poitiers
Metternich – The Passionate Diplomat

Sociology:

You in the Home	Etiquette
The Fascinating Forties	The Many Facets of Love
Marriage for Moderns	Sex and the Teenager
Be Vivid, Be Vital	The Book of Charm
Love, Life and Sex	Living Together
Vitamins for Vitality	The Youth Secret
Husbands and Wives	The Magic of Honey
Men are Wonderful	The Book of Beauty and Health

Keep Young and Beautiful by Barbara Cartland and Elinor Glyn
Etiquette for Love and Romance
Barbara Cartland's Book of Health

Cookery:

Barbara Cartland's Health Food Cookery Book
Food for Love
Magic of Honey Cookbook
Recipes for Lovers
The Romance of Food

Editor of:

"The Common Problem" by Ronald Cartland (with a preface by the Rt. Hon. the Earl of Selborne, P.C.)
Barbara Cartland's Library of Love
Barbara Cartland's Library of Ancient Wisdom
"Written with Love" Passionate love letters selected by Barbara Cartland

Drama:

Blood Money
French Dressing

Philosophy:

Touch the Stars

Radio Operatta:

The Rose and the Violet (Music by Mark Lubbock). Performed in 1942.

Radio Plays:

The Caged Bird: An episode in the life of Elizabeth Empress of Austria. Performed in 1957.

General:

Barbara Cartland's Book of Useless Information with a Foreword by the Earl Mountbatten of Burma.
(In aid of the United World Colleges)
Love and Lovers (Picture Book)

The Light of Love (Prayer Book)
Barbara Cartland's Scrapbook
(In aid of the Royal Photographic Museum)
Romantic Royal Marriages
Barbara Cartland's Book of Celebrities
Getting Older, Growing Younger
A Year of Royal Days

Verse:

Lines on Life and Love

Music:

An Album of Love Songs sung with the Royal Philharmonic
Orchestra.

Films:

The Flame is Love
A Hazard of Hearts

Cartoons:

Barbara Cartland Romances (Book of Cartoons) has
recently been published in the U.S.A., Great Britain and
other parts of the world.

Children:

A Children's Pop-Up Book: "Princess to the Rescue"

AUTHOR'S NOTE

PEARLS ARE the oldest and most universal of jewels. In the Bible, the Talmud and the Koran they are indicators of wealth.

Before 3,500 B.C., civilised Mideast and Asian Society treasured pearls as supremely valuable possessions. To them they were symbols of purity, chastity and innocence.

Later, through the financial and marketing centre in Bombay, the jewels found their way into Royal collections throughout India, Persia and Egypt.

At the height of the Roman Empire, the historian Suetonius reported that the Roman General Vitellius paid for an entire campaign by selling just one of his mother's earrings.

Pliny the Elder wrote in his *Historia Naturalis* that by the first century B.C.:

". . the richest merchandise of all and the most sovereigne commodity throughout the world are these pearls."

I visited Iran when the Shah was on the throne and in Teheran saw the fantastic collection of jewels which was kept with great security hundreds of feet below ground.

There were huge bowls of sapphires, emeralds and diamonds, and actually *trunks* of pearls worth millions of pounds!

Between 1920 and 1930, however, the whole world of pearls changed as cultured pearls from Japan appeared.

For many centuries the Japanese, and other nations, have

tried to entice oysters to make more and better gems.

The Chinese were first successful with their famous pearl Buddhas, a steady product for the faithful from the 12th to the 20th century.

But it was three Japanese working alone who almost simultaneously discovered the secret of pearl culture which made the whole business possible.

Chapter One

1880

NORITA GOT out of the train at Paddington and found her way to the exit from the station with a little difficulty.

She had never been in London before.

She was expecting it would be busy and overwhelming, but the crowds moving about the station were frightening.

She saw, as she expected, a row of Hackney Carriages for hire.

Going up to the first one she asked timidly if he could take her to Hawk House in Park Lane.

"'Op in, Miss!" the coachman said cheerily. "Oi'll get y'there in a jiffy!"

She looked young, and was also very pretty.

He therefore got down from his seat to open the door for her.

"Keep the winders closed, an' yer'll be warm enough," he said. "We're not smart enough to run to a rug!"

He laughed at his own joke and climbed back onto the box to urge his tired horse forward.

To Norita it was very exciting.

She looked through the windows at the small houses that surrounded Paddington. She thought they were somewhat dilapidated and in need of paint.

Then when they came to Hyde Park she saw the trees and the large, luxurious houses in Park Lane.

1

She stared at them entranced.

This was how she had thought London would look, and she was not disappointed.

Hawk House was where she knew she would find the person she was seeking.

It was certainly very impressive, with a drive running from the street up to the front door and out through another gate.

There was a large portico supported by stone columns.

As soon as the carriage pulled up a footman came out of the house to open the door.

"Is this the house of the Marquis of Hawkhurst?" Norita asked.

"Yes, Madam."

She stepped out of the carriage and, as the coachman got down again, she opened her purse.

"How much do I owe you?" she asked in her soft voice.

She paid him what he required, adding sixpence which she thought was the right tip, and was sure it was when he took off his cap saying:

"Thanks, Miss! It's bin a pleasure t'drive yer 'ere!"

She gave him a shy little smile, and said to the footman:

"I have called to see Miss Marsh."

"Is she expecting you, Madam?" the footman enquired.

"I think so. I wrote to her two days ago, and she should have had the letter by now."

Two other footmen who were in the hall stood listening, and Norita had the frightening feeling they might turn her away.

Then one, who appeared to be a little older than the others, said:

"You'll find Miss Marsh in th' School-Room, Madam. She did tell Mr. Bates that she were expectin' somebody."

Norita gave a little sigh of relief.

She followed the footman who was wearing a very smart livery, up an important-looking staircase.

She felt almost too nervous to look round, but she was aware that the walls were hung with portraits in gold frames.

The marble mantelpiece was a fine example of 18th century carving.

She wished she could tell her father about it.

Then, as they reached the top of the staircase, the footman turned left, and a few seconds later they climbed a very different stairway.

The walls were hung with watercolours rather than oils.

There was another landing, and yet another staircase until at last they were on the top floor.

Here the ceilings were lower.

But the winter sunshine coming through the windows seemed to give the place a glow.

The footman opened a door that was painted and not the mahogany of those they had passed on the way up.

"A visitor t'see you, Miss Marsh!" he announced.

With an exclamation of delight Norita ran towards an elderly woman who was rising from a chair by the fire.

She held out her hands but Norita flung her arms around her and kissed her.

"Oh, Marshy!" she said, "I am so glad to see you! I was so afraid you would not be here."

"I was delighted to get your letter," Miss Marsh replied, "but you have not come to London alone?"

"There was no one to come with me," Norita said, "and I am not a child. I managed to find my way to you without any trouble."

"But you should certainly not have come unattended," Miss Marsh remarked in a voice that showed she was shocked at the idea.

Then before Norita could speak she said:

"But you are here and that is all that matters. Take off your coat, dear, and luncheon will be up soon."

Norita did as she was told, putting her coat, which was warm but old-fashioned, on a chair and adding her small, plain felt hat.

She looked slim and very young as she moved back to the fireplace to say:

"It was crowded on the train, but I travelled First Class because I thought that as I was alone, it would be the right thing to do."

"Of course it was!" Miss Marsh agreed.

"But it is very expensive," Norita sighed, "and unless you can help me, I do not have enough money for my return fare."

Miss Marsh stared at her in astonishment.

"What do you mean? What are you telling me?"

Norita was still for a moment. Until, looking into the fire, she said:

"Papa . . died a week . . ago."

"Died?" Miss Marsh echoed. "It was not in the newspapers."

"I could not faford to send a notice to *The Morning Post*."

"But how did it happen? I do not understand."

"It was a new horse that Papa bought. He was very wild . . but . . Papa thought . . he could . . train him."

Norita gave a little sob before she went on:

"He . . threw Papa . . then rolled on . . top of him!"

"Oh, dearest child, I am so sorry!" Miss Marsh exclaimed.

"I suppose," Norita said in a very small voice, "it was better that Papa died while he was still unconscious because the doctors said if he had lived he . . would have been . . paralysed."

As she spoke she took a handkerchief from her bag and wiped her eyes.

Then she sat down on the rug in front of the fire saying:

"It has all been so horrible, Marshy, like a terrible nightmare, and now that Papa is dead . . there is no . . money!"

4

"What do you mean by that?" Miss Marsh asked. "I always knew your father and mother were poor, but. . ."

"After Mama died," Norita interrupted, "I suppose Papa and I were rather extravagant, and the horses did not sell as well as they should."

She looked up at Miss Marsh.

There was a pleading expression in her eyes as she said:

"I have realised that I have to find some work to do, and that is why I have come to you."

"Work?" Miss Marsh repeated. "How can you possibly work?"

Norita gave a choked little laugh.

"I either have to work or starve and, quite frankly, I do not like being hungry."

"I cannot believe what you are saying," Miss Marsh exclaimed.

"It is true," Norita insisted, "and because the Cosnets are too old to find another job it would be much easier to let them stay at the house and give them a small pension."

Miss Marsh was silent, and Norita went on:

"I have thought it all out very carefully, just as you taught me to do. The Cosnets think they can manage on seven shillings a week with what they can grow in the garden."

Norita looked into the fire as if she was seeing the accounts in the flames as she went on:

"If I could earn just enough money to keep them and did not have to pay for my own food, then I should always have a home to go to if I was incompetent and got the sack!"

She gave a little laugh as if it was funny, but Miss Marsh was looking very serious.

"Dearest child," she said, "you are only just eighteen. What could you possibly do to earn money?"

"It is something I have to do," Norita said, "and there is no other way of living, unless I send the Cosnets to the Workhouse, which would break their hearts! I could sell the house, but I think it would be very difficult!"

Miss Marsh knew this was the truth.

Norita's home — The Manor — was at the end of the small village of Berkhampstead.

It was in the unfashionable part of Hertfordshire and it was hard to imagine anyone would want to pay much for the house.

Which when she had last seen it was in a very dilapidated state.

The diamond-paned windows might be Elizabethan, the bricks mellowed with age a beautiful pink, but the roof was badly in need of repair.

She remembered Norita's mother, Lady Wyncombe, saying:

"We have had to shut up the top floor completely. Anyone who sleeps there has a bath every time it rains!"

She laughed as if it was of no particular consequence.

Miss Marsh had thought then that no one else could take the difficulties of life so lightly.

Nor be so happy in what, to say the least of it, were uncomfortable circumstances.

Lord and Lady Wyncombe had married each other because they were in love.

It had been an alliance which had received for both of them the disapproval of their relatives.

That did not trouble them in the slightest.

They were supremely happy, living in the country with the horses which Lord Wyncombe broke in and sold for a great deal more than he paid for them.

They adored their only child, Norita, whose beauty seemed an expression of their love.

Miss Marsh had, owing to a small Legacy, retired early from a life of teaching.

She rented a small cottage in the village where her father had been the Schoolmaster.

When Lady Wyncombe had begged her to teach Norita, she had found it an interest and a pleasure.

She was not concerned with the fact that she received very little money for it.

It had been a delight to go to a house which always seemed to be filled with sunshine.

To be with people who were so happy that they made everything around them seem a part of their own joy of living.

Miss Marsh, who was a very intelligent woman, had given Norita some of her lessons.

While she had others from the Schoolmaster and the Vicar.

No one could resist Lady Wyncombe when she pleaded for something.

All three of Norita's Tutors considered it a joy rather than a task.

Miss Marsh loved Norita.

It had never entered her head that she would ever be reduced to earning her own living.

She had left the village a year ago because the Dowager Marchioness of Hawkhurst, whose daughters she had taught, had begged her, if only for a short time, to look after her grand-daughter.

After several comfortable years of retirement, Miss Marsh had no wish to resume her profession.

But the Dowager Marchioness had always been extremely kind to her and was very persistent.

"Only you, Miss Marsh, can help the child," she had written flatteringly.

She was also offered a very large salary that it would have been impossible for Miss Marsh to refuse.

Now, she had informed the Marquis's Secretary, Mr. Seymour, that she had to leave as soon as he could find somebody to take her place.

"My elder sister has just lost her husband," she explained. "She is in ill health herself, and there is no one to look after her."

7

She paused before she went on:

"So you will understand, Mr. Seymour, that although I hate to leave Lady Alyce, blood is thicker than water."

"So I have always heard, Miss Marsh," Mr. Seymour replied dryly. "At the same time, I know Lady Alyce will miss you, and it will be very upsetting for all of us to try and find somebody to take your place."

Miss Marsh had made a helpless little gesture with her hand, but there was nothing he could do, and she merely said:

"Please, Mr. Seymour, find somebody as quickly as you can. My sister is really ill and needs me."

It was just fortunate, she told herself, that she was here when Norita came to see her.

Otherwise she would have left for Devonshire and the child could not possibly have travelled all that way alone.

Nor would she have had the money to do so.

"I knew you would be able to tell me what I could do," Norita was saying, "and no one knows my talents better, if I have any!"

"Of course you have a great number," Miss Marsh said, "but none that are particularly saleable."

Norita laughed.

"If that is true, then all I can say is that you, that nice Mr. Tomlinson and the Vicar should be ashamed of yourselves! You used to give glowing reports to Papa of my progress, and he was very proud of me, and so was Mama!"

Miss Marsh did not answer, and after a moment Norita said:

"Papa always said I was a very good rider, but I do not think I could break in horses like he did."

"Of course not!" Miss Marsh cried. "You are far too small and I never did think it was a suitable task for a woman!"

"I was thinking about it when I was in the train," Norita said, "and that leaves only two things."

8

"What are they?" Miss Marsh enquired.

"I can look after small children, or become companion to some cantankerous old lady!"

Miss Marsh was staring at her with a sudden alertness in her eyes.

"What is it?" Norita asked. "What are you thinking?"

"It has only just occurred to me," Miss Marsh said, "but perhaps, although it might be a mistake, you could take my place."

"Take your place?" Norita enquired. "But, why?"

"I am leaving here. I have to go and look after my sister who is very ill. You remember Ethel, I used to tell you about her."

"Yes, of course I remember her, and I am very sorry to hear that she is ill," Norita said.

"I informed Mr. Seymour only yesterday morning that he had to find somebody to take my place as quickly as possible."

"Who is Mr. Seymour?" Norita enquired.

"He is His Lordship's secretary and runs this house and Hawk Hall in Oxfordshire."

"You wrote and told me how beautiful it was there," Norita said. "I used to love reading about the swans on the lake and the fountain that played in the garden."

She spoke dreamily, then she said in a different tone of voice:

"Do you really mean I could look after the little girl who is your pupil and live at Hawk Hall?"

"You are too young," Miss Marsh said, but her voice was not very positive.

"Oh, please, Marshy, do not say that!" Norita pleaded. "After all, you always said I was very intelligent for my age, and I am sure I could teach her nearly as well as you taught me!"

"It is not that," Miss Marsh said.

"Then . . what is it?"

9

"You should not be alone at your age, unchaperoned and unprotected."

"Why should I want protecting if I am at Hawk Hall?" Norita asked.

Miss Marsh did not reply. Then she said as if she was speaking to herself:

"You should be all right. After all, there is no reason for you to come in contact with anybody outside the School-Room. I never have!"

Norita looked at her in perplexity.

As if she was trying to think, Miss Marsh put her hand up to her forehead in a familiar gesture and closed her eyes.

She was seeing almost as if he was standing in front of her the handsome, rather dissolute, and very cynical face of the Marquis of Hawkhurst.

He had, she was well aware, a charm when he wished to use it.

As the servants always said, it 'mesmerised any woman who looked at him'.

His reputation as a sportsman received the admiration of all the menservants in his houses and on his estates.

It was women servants who whispered about his love-affairs and eulogised over his handsome looks and the way no Lady could resist him.

"They runs after 'im like bees round a honeypot!" one of the house-maids had said to Miss Marsh only last week.

It was not an original remark for she had heard it many times before.

"You should not discuss His Lordship's private affairs, Amy," she had replied seriously.

"Aw, go on wiv yer!" Amy replied. "You knows as well as I does that there's nothing else to talk about in this place 'cept His Lordship!"

Miss Marsh had thought it beneath her dignity to reply.

It was from the Housekeeper with whom she was friendly that she had heard that His Lordship's last 'Fancy', an outstanding Beauty, had been discarded.

The latest, Lady Bettine Daviot, was the daughter of a Duke.

Her picture appeared in *The Lady Magazine* and many other illustrated periodicals.

"She's mad about him, I hear," Mrs. Winter the House-keeper went on, "and Mr. Newman heard two gentlemen saying that the betting at White's Club is 20–1 against it lasting more than two months."

"I do not understand," Miss Marsh had said disdainfully, "why it is that gentlemen have nothing better to do than to talk gossip. I had always believed it was a woman's prerogative."

Mrs. Winter had laughed.

"If you ask me, Miss Marsh, they're all jealous of His Lordship because he's such a success. He wins on the racecourse, he wins the most beautiful ladies, and he wins, hands downs, when it comes to looks!"

That was certainly true, Miss Marsh thought.

His Lordship was extremely handsome and he was also enormously rich, and because he was a widower, he was obviously the most eligible *partie* in the whole of Society.

How, she asked herself now, could she allow Norita — so young, unsophisticated and very innocent — to enter his world, that shocked a great number of people?

It would, she knew, if she was alive, have shocked Lady Wyncombe.

Then she told herself it was doubtful if Norita would ever come in contact with the Marquis.

Since she had been in his employment she had hardly ever seen him from one month to another.

When Alyce had been sent for to go downstairs and see her father, the child went alone.

He had made it clear that he was not particularly interested in talking to her.

Sometimes he would be a week or even more at Hawk

Hall before he sent for the child.

Then she would stay in his company for not more than ten minutes.

Miss Marsh thought it heartless but she was aware that Alyce was not a particularly prepossessing child.

She seemed to have little energy.

None of the high spirits Miss Marsh had found in Norita and the other children she had taught.

At eight years of age, Lady Alyce would sit quietly in the School-Room, not playing with her toys, but just sitting looking at them.

She liked being read to, but she did not complain when Miss Marsh was too busy to do so.

At her lessons she seemed to be extraordinarily stupid.

Miss Marsh, if she was honest, had to admit that she had taught the child very little, and her only excuse was that she could not arouse her interest in anything.

"I will be very glad to leave here," she told herself.

Then she thought of her large salary.

She knew, if she was truthful, the money was welcome.

She had saved most of it for when she finally retired.

With the money she had already she could be very comfortable, far more so than she had been before.

She knew that if Norita tried to get employment in any other place, it would be difficult because she was so young.

She would also not receive even half the amount of money she had received herself because the Dowager Marchioness had insisted upon it.

Then once again she remembered the Marquis and told herself, however, he was far too conscious of his own importance to concern himself with a Governess, however attractive she might be!

Miss Marsh made up her mind and bent towards Norita.

"Now listen, my dear," she said, "I will go and speak to Mr. Seymour about your taking my place here."

Norita gave a little cry of excitement and clasped her

hands together.

"Do you mean that, Marshy? Do you really mean it?"

"I mean it," Miss Marsh said. "At the same time, listen to me, because this is important!"

"I am listening," Norita answered.

"If you come here, no one is to know who you are."

"Why not?"

"Because it would be a great mistake for anyone to know you are a Lady, and that you have a title, even though it is a small one."

"I . . I do not understand."

Miss Marsh chose her words carefully.

"It would be embarrassing if it was known who you are, first for the servants, who would feel uncomfortable that you really belong to the front of the house."

Norita smiled, but she did not interrupt and Miss Marsh continued:

"Secondly, it might also be uncomfortable for His Lordship and for his guests."

She hesitated for a moment. Then she went on:

"A Governess has a rather difficult position in life, and my father used to say I am 'neither flesh, fowl, nor good red herring!'"

Norita laughed, and it was a very pretty sound.

"I remember Papa saying that once."

"It is true," Miss Marsh said. "You are in a 'No-Man's Land' between the Drawing-Room and the Servants' Hall, and that, Norita, is where you have to stay. Do you understand?"

"Of course I understand," Norita replied, "and I shall be quite happy in a lovely School-Room like this where I see you have plenty of books."

She looked as she spoke at the shelves which nearly covered one side of the room.

"There are certainly plenty of them," Miss Marsh remarked, "and the Library at Hawk Hall is enormous and when the Marquis is not at home, I am sure his Curator would be delighted for you to browse for as long as you like, but listen, Norita — this is important!"

"I am listening."

"When the Marquis is in residence you must never — never! — do you understand? — go to the front of the house! You will stay in the School-Room, you will take Lady Alyce out by a side door, and if you ride with her. . ."

"You mean . . I can ride the Marquis's horses?" Norita interrupted.

"Of course you can ride, if you want to," Miss Marsh said. "It is something I never cared for, but as I was saying, you must not ride when the Marquis is at home. If Lady Alyce wishes to ride, you must send a groom with her instead."

'What you are saying," Norita said, "is that I am not to meet him."

"Exactly!" Miss Marsh replied. "But if you do, just curtsey and take his orders, then move away from him as quickly as possible."

"You make him sound contagious!"

"If you will not promise me that you will do exactly as I have told you," Miss Marsh warned in a repressive tone, "I will not recommend you to Mr. Seymour in my place."

"I promise! I promise!" Norita cried. "Oh, Marshy, I knew you would save me, and I really felt desperate until I thought of coming to you."

"I only hope I am doing the right thing," Miss Marsh said doubtfully. "Now stay here while I go and talk to Mr. Seymour. It is best if he does not see you until everything is agreed, otherwise, I am sure he will think you are too young."

"I will hide under the sofa until you come back!" Norita teased.

"Now, Norita, do be sensible!" Miss Marsh pleaded. "I am trying to help you, but I am so afraid that it will be

14

something of which your father and certainly your mother would disapprove."

"They would not approve of my starving to death at home, and sending the Cosnets to the Workhouse!"

Norita clasped her hands together again as she said:

"Oh, Marshy, you do not know how frightened I have been thinking of what the Cosnets would have to do, and I know by the way they look and the pleading in their eyes how much the idea terrifies them!"

Miss Marsh got to her feet.

"Now just stay there," she said, "and do not make a noise or you will wake Lady Alyce."

"Where is she?"

"In her bedroom next door," Miss Marsh replied. "You can go and peep in at her, and if she is awake, talk to her, but the doctor says she is to rest as much as possible."

"I will certainly have a look at her," Norita said.

Miss Marsh went away.

Rising, Norita walked across the room. There was a door which obviously led into what had been the Night Nursery.

She looked in cautiously.

In a very elaborate, very attractive bed draped with muslin curtains there was a small girl.

She had straight dark hair which fell lightly on either side of her very pale face.

Her eyes were open and she was staring at the ceiling while her hands lay limply on either side of the sheets.

"Hello!" Norita said.

The child seemed to slowly focus her eyes on Norita, and there was no expression of surprise in them.

"May I come in and talk to you?" Norita asked.

As she spoke she walked towards the bed and sat down on the side of it.

"I have been talking to Miss Marsh," she said, "and she tells me she has to go away to look after her sister who is very ill."

15

Lady Alyce did not seem perturbed by this information, and Norita went on:

"She thought perhaps you would like to have me to look after you in her place. What do you think about it?"

There seemed to be a little more interest in Lady Alyce's eyes, before in a rather flat voice she asked:

"Are you a Governess?"

"I am going to try to be one," Norita answered, "but you will have to help me."

"Help you?"

"Yes, you will have to tell me what to do and make sure I do not teach you the wrong things. I have never been a Governess before, and it is going to be difficult until I get used to it."

"And I can tell you all the things I want to do?"

"It would make things much easier than my having to guess," Norita replied.

The child seemed to consider this. Then she said:

"Suppose I want to do nothing?"

Norita smiled.

"That will be all right. When you want to do nothing I will read, and I love reading."

"And what about lessons?"

"Perhaps you could think of the lessons you like to do best, then we could talk about them," Norita said.

She saw that Lady Alyce was regarding her speculatively as if she thought she was very strange, so Norita said:

"We could do extraordinary lessons which are different from those anyone has ever done before, and what I often wanted to do when I was a child, but nobody would let me."

She smiled before she continued:

"I had to sit at the table and write things down in a book instead of exploring in the woods, or trying to see if there was a nymph in the river."

"What is a nymph?" Lady Alyce asked.

"A nymph is a kind of water fairy," Norita answered.

"You know, there are fairies in the flowers?"

"I have never .. seen one."

"Then you cannot have looked properly," Norita replied. "I am sure I have seen them. I have, too, seen the fairies dancing in the moonlight and in the morning they leave a ring of toadstools to show where they have danced."

"I do not believe you!" Lady Alyce exclaimed. "It is not true!"

"To me it is," Norita said, "and I am sure we could find some pictures of fairies in the books in the Library if we search for them."

Lady Alyce considered this for some minutes.

Then she said:

"I do not want to write about fairies in a book."

"You could not do that, unless you had seen them," Norita said.

"I .. think I have .. seen them," Lady Alyce replied, "but they are secret .. very .. very .. secret!"

Norita felt this was a clue to the child that somehow seemed important.

She lowered her voice.

"If it is a secret," she said, "we must only talk about it when there is no chance of anybody hearing us."

Lady Alyce nodded as if this was logical.

Then she asked:

"Are you really coming to be my Governess?"

"If you want me," Norita replied. "I would be unhappy if you did not want me and I could not talk to you secretly."

There was what seemed a long pause before Lady Alyce said:

"I want you! Tell Miss Marsh I want you!"

* * *

Downstairs, Mr. Seymour was saying delightedly:

"You know, Miss Marsh, I will be only too pleased to accept anyone on your recommendation."

17

"It is just fortunate that Miss Combe has come to see me unexpectedly," Miss Marsh said. "She is young, Mr. Seymour, but I cannot help thinking that is what Lady Alyce needs; someone very much younger than I am to be with her, and to stimulate her into taking more interest in life than she does at the moment."

"I am sure you are right," Mr. Seymour said, "and it really is a great relief to me at this moment, when I am so busy with His Lordship's affairs, not to have to spend time interviewing what I am sure would be a great number of women who would be quite unsuitable."

"Then I need not take up any more of your time, Mr. Seymour," Miss Marsh replied. "I will tell Miss Combe to come here the day after tomorrow, if that suits you, then I can leave for my sister who is really very ill."

"I am quite content to leave everything in your very capable hands, Miss Marsh, and I presume Miss Combe will accept the same salary as you have been getting?"

"Yes, I think she would accept that," Miss Marsh agreed, "but what I would like, Mr. Seymour, is to give her some money for the journey back to Berkhampstead, and of course for her return journey on Wednesday with her luggage."

She waited while Mr. Seymour unlocked a drawer of his desk and counted out five golden sovereigns.

"I think that should be enough, Miss Marsh, unless you think Miss Combe will require more?"

"No, I am sure she can manage," Miss Marsh replied, "and thank you."

"Thank you very much indeed!" Mr. Seymour said. "I really am up to my eyes at the moment, and this is a great weight off my mind!"

Miss Marsh left him and returned to the School-Room.

As she entered, Norita was just coming out of Lady Alyce's bedroom.

"I thought I heard you coming up the stairs," she said.

She shut the child's door behind her. Then she asked anxiously:

"Is it all right?"

"It is all right, my dear, and Mr. Seymour is too busy to see you, which is a relief, and has also agreed that you should have the same salary as I am getting."

"How much is that?" Norita asked.

"£50 a year," Miss Marsh replied.

"As much as that?" Norita asked. "Oh, Marshy, how wonderful! I will be able to let the Cosnets stay, and there will be no need for me to worry about them."

"No need at all," Miss Marsh said, "and here is the money for your fare. You are to return here the day after tomorrow, and please make it as early as possible in the morning."

"Of course I will do that," Norita replied.

"I have already arranged," Miss Marsh went on, "that a housemaid will go with you to the Station and see you into a carriage reserved for ladies only. You will return on Wednesday. I know there is a train that gets in at about eleven o'clock. There will be a carriage waiting for you, and one of the footmen to see to your luggage."

Norita laughed and put her arms around Miss Marsh's neck.

"I shall feel like a Royal Princess at the very least," she said, "and thank you, thank you, Marshy! You have been wonderful, and I can never thank you enough!"

"I only hope you will be all right," Miss Marsh said in a slightly worried tone.

"Of course I shall!" Norita answered, "and I will try very hard to make Lady Alyce happy."

She kissed Miss Marsh again and put on her hat and coat.

Miss Marsh took her downstairs.

They had almost reached the Ground Floor when Norita stopped and said:

"You said I was not to mention Papa or Mama. Do I have to change my name?"

"There is no need to do that," Miss Marsh said. "There are plenty of Combes in the world, so it is not a name that is unusual."

"I will be careful," Norita promised, "and I must say, I prefer using my own name. It is so much easier to remember!"

She laughed.

Then she hurried down to where an elderly housemaid was waiting.

* * *

The following morning the Marquis was sitting in his Study.

He was looking at the pile of letters his Secretary had left on the left-hand side of his gold-cornered blotter.

He knew that Seymour, with his usual tact, had been aware that these were personal.

He therefore had not opened them as he did all the rest of his master's correspondence.

The Marquis turned them over one by one with the tip of his finger.

He recognised Melinda's writing which was very flowery, Daisy's hand was much neater.

There was no mistaking the scent of gardenias which Eileen used too heavily on her writing-paper.

He found the letter he wanted which was from Bettine Daviot, and opened it with a faint smile on his rather hard lips.

As he did so, a voice from the door announced:

"Sir William Smithson to see you, M'Lord!"

The Marquis looked up.

He saw the Royal Doctor, who had been given the K.C.V.O. in the last Honours List, was approaching him.

He then remembered what he had been told by his Secretary.

The Governess had asked for his daughter to have a

Specialist's opinion about her health.

He wondered vaguely why it was necessary as he held out his hand to Sir William.

"Nice to see you, My Lord," Sir William said, "and there is no need to ask how you are! I have never seen you in better health!"

"I feel well, thank Heaven!" the Marquis replied. "But I understand that my daughter's Governess wanted your expert opinion."

He indicated a chair, adding as he did so:

"Do sit down."

"I cannot stay for long," Sir William said. "I am due at Marlborough House. Princess Alexandra has one of her sore throats, and sent for me to 'nip it in the bud', so to speak!"

"Very sensible!" the Marquis approved, "but what is wrong with Alyce?"

"You will allow me to speak frankly?" Sir William enquired.

"Naturally!" the Marquis answered dryly.

"Then, in my opinion, the child is anaemic, and is also suffering from the intense cold we have endured this winter."

"It has been cold," the Marquis admitted. "But we have burnt an enormous amount of coal."

"What is really bad for her is the air Lady Alyce breathes outside the house," Sir William said. "What I am going to suggest, My Lord, is that you send her immediately to a warmer climate, otherwise, I am afraid she might get an infection of the lungs which could be serious."

"A warmer climate?" the Marquis repeated as if he had never heard of such a place.

"If I was talking to someone who could not afford it, I realise it would be difficult," Sir William said with a smile, "but it should not raise any problems for you, My Lord."

He paused to go on with a twinkle in his eye:

"Especially when you have a new yacht which the Prince of Wales is afraid is going to be faster and more impressive than the *Britannia*!"

The Marquis laughed.

"Are you telling me that is worrying His Royal Highness?"

"Of course it is," Sir William replied. "You know he is jealous of anyone who excels in his special sport."

"That makes it rather difficult," the Marquis remarked. "I am very pleased with my latest acquisition."

"I am sure you are, and from all I hear it is big enough for you to house a hundred children without your being aware of them."

There was a slight frown between the Marquis's eyes as he said:

"Actually, I was thinking, now that hunting is over, of taking the *Sea Hawk* to the sun."

"Excellent!" Sir William remarked. "Take Lady Alyce with you, and I am quite sure by the time you return she will be a different child!"

He glanced at the clock and rose to his feet.

"The sunshine, new interests, these are better tonics than anything I can prescribe."

He held out his hand as he spoke.

"Thank you for coming," the Marquis said, "and I shall certainly consider your advice and try to include Alyce in my party, although she is a little young."

The Marquis twisted his lips as he spoke, which told Sir William exactly what the party would be like.

Also that the Marquis was well aware it was what he expected.

"Enjoy yourself!" Sir William said, "and put Lady Alyce into the hold and forget about her!"

He laughed again as the Marquis escorted him politely into the hall and the Butler showed him into his brougham which was waiting outside.

The Marquis walked back to his Study.

Only as the footman hurried to open the door for him did he say sharply:

"Send Mr. Seymour to me!"

Chapter Two

THE MARQUIS of Hawkhurst drove his Phaeton down Park Lane, aware as he did so that the passers-by stood and stared.

It was certainly a spectacular turnout.

The Phaeton was painted black with yellow wheels, and the pair of black-and-blood horses who drew it were without a patch of colour on their bodies.

The Marquis sported a yellow carnation in his button-hole.

With his hat on the side of his dark head, every woman who looked at him felt her heart was beating a little faster.

He was on his way to call on Lady Bettine Daviot, and he had with him a present which he thought would please her.

Lady Bettine was an acknowledged Beauty before the Marquis had met her.

Since their fiery *affaire de coeur* had started her beauty had increased.

She had been married when she was very young to a man far older than herself. She had never lost her heart until she met the Marquis.

She was, however, spoilt by the admiration she had received almost since she left the School-Room.

Her impulsive nature would obviously become more passionate as she grew older.

Her parents therefore had quickly married her off to the most important suitor of her first Season in London.

Lord Daviot belonged to a family who could trace their

24

ancestors back nine centuries.

In fact to before the arrival of William the Conqueror on the shores of Great Britain, and he was extremely wealthy.

That he was also very mean did not emerge until after they were married.

Then Lady Bettine found his cheese-paring on a number of things, which included herself, extremely irritating.

By the time she was twenty-five she had collected an amusing Court of friends.

They praised everything she did, and paid her flowery compliments, which she considered her right.

The first lovers she took were slightly disappointing.

Only when she succumbed to the Marquis's irresistible attraction did she understand the meaning of the word 'Love'.

She had actually pursued him because other women spoke so glowingly of him.

She was determined to capture him as it would be an unrivalled 'feather in her cap'.

That she had fallen in love was unexpected.

She resented the way she yearned for him and waited breathlessly for him to accept her invitations.

It was not difficult for her to have a *liaison*.

Lord Daviot spent his time in their large country house in Hampshire or else, when the season was right, shooting and fishing.

He was quite content for his wife to grace his table, to wear the Daviot jewels and entertain his friends.

They were all about the same age as himself, and their conversation was confined to sport.

If His Lordship suspected that Lady Bettine was unfaithful to him, he never accused her of it.

Nor did it seem to perturb him that she was constantly surrounded by men far younger than himself.

This, from Lady Bettine's point of view, was an ideal situation and she made the very most of it.

Lord Daviot was at the moment at their country house concerned with his duties as Lord Lieutenant of the County, and consulting with his gamekeepers.

Daviot House in Belgrave Square was, therefore, filled with Lady Bettine's personal friends. They were all the most attractive women of her own age.

They came with men who did little in their lives, except move from *Boudoir* to *Boudoir*.

"I saw your latest conquest last night," the Countess of Dorset, one of Lady Bettine's closest friends, remarked.

There was no doubt about the envy in the Countess's silky voice, and there was also an undoubted glint of antagonism in her green eyes.

"I cannot think who you mean," Lady Bettine replied evasively.

"You are well aware that I am referring to the elusive Marquis," the Countess answered, "and I am afraid, dearest, like everyone else, that is what you will find him!"

"Thank you for the warning," Lady Bettine replied.

She was well aware that the Countess had pursued the Marquis and failed to capture him.

She could not help, therefore, saying a little spitefully:

"It is so fortunate that Selwyn always seems to prefer fair women."

The Countess, whose hair was dark, turned away with a flounce, but not before she said:

"There are exceptions to every rule!"

Lady Bettine laughed to herself.

Last night the Marquis had convinced her that she was everything he desired in a woman.

She was sure that no man could be such an ardent and exciting lover unless that was true.

Her guests left to go on to another Reception very much the same as hers. She walked to the gold-framed mirror in her elegant Drawing-Room to look at her reflection.

She was just as beautiful, she thought, as every man told her she was.

Her hair was the gold of ripening corn, her skin the perfect pink-and-white which only Englishwomen seemed to achieve.

Her lips, which no man could resist, were red and inviting.

"I am beautiful! I am very beautiful!" she told herself.

It was something she had discovered when she was quite young, and when she looked at a man provocatively from under her eyelashes they longed to kiss her.

She did not particularly enjoy their kisses or the fact that they wanted to touch her.

What she adored was the feeling of power.

The knowledge that a man was caught like a rat in a trap, and she could manipulate him as she wished.

She expected men to give her expensive presents and made sure that they did. It was part of the spoils of victory.

She could persuade her husband, if she tried hard enough, into giving her furs and jewellery.

But it was hard work and so much easier to obtain everything she wanted from those who were more open-handed.

Now, she thought with a smile, she would persuade the Marquis to buy her a diamond necklace she had seen at her Jewellers.

It was astronomically expensive, but he could afford it.

What was more, it was only right that he should pay for the flames of passion she lit inside him.

And she was sure she had made them burn more brilliantly than any other woman had ever managed to achieve.

She knew she would see him in a very short time, and she smoothed her hair, added a touch of salve to her lips and a little powder to her classically shaped nose.

Then she smiled at herself appreciatively.

Moving from the Drawing-Room she went into the small, comfortable Sitting-Room where she received her most intimate friends.

The room was fragrant with the scent of hot-house flowers.

The winter sunshine coming feebly through the windows, glinted golden on a profusion of small ornaments.

They glittered on every table, some of them bejewelled, many of them gold, a few of silver.

They were all little tributes that Lady Bettine had received from her admirers.

Their more appreciated offerings were in the large Jewel-Box surmounted by a Coronet, which she kept in a safe.

She settled herself carefully on a sofa, lifting her bustle to do so.

She made sure that her tightly-fitting bodice, which showed every curve of her perfect figure, was not creased.

Her waist was tiny, and she thought with satisfaction that her maid had been able to lace up her corset nearly half-an-inch tighter this week.

It was the result of a strict control over what she ate.

While feeling at times desperately hungry, Lady Bettine hoped the Marquis would appreciate the effort she made on his behalf.

"I love the smallness of your waist," he had said two days ago as he put his hands around it and nearly managed to make them meet.

He then pulled her close to him and kissed her until she was breathless.

Yet always, after he had left her, Lady Bettine remembered that he had never, as other men did, said that he loved her.

He complimented her face, her figure and the way she dressed.

She knew instinctively that she had not completely captured his heart.

She would, however, never have admitted it, even to her most intimate friends.

She often suspected that when he left her, even after their most passionate hours of love-making, he was not thinking of her.

It was not that she thought he was unfaithful to her.

She had always been told that the Marquis concentrated on one woman at a time, and one woman only.

She had also learnt that, unfortunately, his concentration did not last for long.

Almost before they could believe it possible, his attention had been diverted by another pretty face and he was gone.

"That will not happen to me!" Lady Bettine said firmly with a hard look in her sky-blue eyes and a tightening of her Cupid's-bow lips.

The door opened and the Butler announced:

"The Marquis of Hawkhurst, M'Lady!"

Lady Bettine gave a well-simulated cry of surprise.

At the same time, she felt her heart leap in a manner which had never been achieved by any other man.

"How lovely to see you!" she said holding out her hands.

She did not rise to her feet, but waited for the Marquis to take in the picture she made.

She was framed by the silk cushions and the blue damask of the sofa on which she was sitting which matched her eyes. She might have stepped out of a picture by Fragonar.

She knew that no man could be more handsome, no man look more exciting.

There was about the Marquis a raffish look, which made women think of him as a pirate or a buccaneer.

There was also, despite the cynical twist to his lips, a distinct twinkle in his grey eyes, and he was well aware that Lady Bettine was putting on an act.

At the same time, he appreciated that it was a very professional performance.

He bent to kiss her hand, then her fingers tightened on his

and she stood up beside him.

"I was hoping you would not forget me."

The words were wistful, but there was just a faint note in her voice which proclaimed that it was quite impossible for him to do so.

"I have brought you a present," the Marquis said.

"A present?" Lady Bettine exclaimed. "How delightful! And how very sweet of you!"

"I hope you will think so," he replied.

He handed her, as he spoke, a small pink Jewel-box. She was aware it came from one of the most expensive Jewellers in Bond Street.

She opened the lid, then there was just a slight pause before she said:

"A brooch? A pearl brooch! How — pretty!"

Lying in the velvet interior of the box was an exquisite replica of two small bunches of grapes, fashioned in pearls.

The leaves which held them in gold were so life-like as to be almost incredible.

There was complete silence as Lady Bettine examined it. Then the Marquis said:

"It is a clever piece of craftsmanship, but I can see you do not like it."

"The pearls are a little — small!" Lady Bettine said hesitatingly.

The Marquis took the box from her hands, and closed the lid. Then he put it down on a side-table.

"I will buy you something else."

"I would like anything that you gave me," Lady Bettine said. "At the same time, if I am to have pearls, I do, dear Selwyn, like them to be — large!"

"But of course!" the Marquis replied.

He was thinking that he might have guessed that Bettine would not appreciate the immense amount of work which had gone into the pearl brooch.

It was a masterpiece of its kind.

He had thought it was one of the most attractive pieces of jewellery he had even seen in England.

When he had been in Paris, he had appreciated the marvellous work of Oscar Massin.

The Frenchman designed the most original and brilliant pieces of jewellery anyone had ever seen.

There were flowers, like lilies-of-the valley, in pearls and diamonds that seemed almost life-like.

At the end of the Second Empire, Frenchwomen coveted jewels that looked like flowers, or fruit.

He suspected that the bunch of grapes he had bought for Lady Bettine were of French origin. They had definitely been made early in the century.

It was a delight to his eye, but he told himself that, beautiful though Bettine was, her knowledge of art of any sort was very small.

He would therefore buy her something sparkling which she would really prefer.

Lady Bettine's arms were already pulling his lips down to hers.

"Thank you, darling Selwyn," she said, "for thinking of me. I am not ungrateful."

"I do not want you to be disappointed," he said, "and so I have an idea."

She was ready for him to kiss her.

But because she was curious she asked:

"What is it?"

As she asked the question she was wondering how, without sounding too greedy, she could mention a diamond necklace she had seen.

"Because I think pearls would become you," the Marquis replied, "and also because you want them to be large, I suggest we go and find what you require at the source from where they come."

Lady Bettine wrinkled the perfect oval of her forehead.

"From where they come?" she asked. "What do you mean by that?"

"I have been trying to think on my way here," the Marquis said, "where I could take you which would be unusual, as well as enjoyable. Now you have given me the answer."

"Which is?"

"Bahrain, in the Persian Gulf!"

Lady Bettine was so surprised that she took her arms from around his neck and stepped back to stare at him.

"What are you saying, Selwyn?" she asked. "I do not understand."

The Marquis put an arm round her and drew her down on the sofa.

"Now listen," he said, "there is no reason why we should stay in this abominable climate, and I also want to try out the *Sea Hawk*."

"Your yacht?" Lady Bettine exclaimed recognising the name. "Oh Selwyn, are you thinking of taking me to the South?"

"I am taking you to the sunshine!" the Marquis said firmly.

It was what Lady Bettine had longed for, but had actually thought it was too soon in the year.

She also suspected the Marquis would prefer to take his new yacht to sea with his male friends.

She had always thought, and perhaps her husband had put the idea into her head, that women at sea were a nuisance.

They would be sea-sick and often bored at being in a confined space for too long a time.

Something else flashed through her mind. If she had the Marquis to herself in a ship from which he could not escape it would be an easy way of holding him captive.

She clasped her hands together, and threw back her head

in a slightly exaggerated manner so as to show the rounded perfection of her neck.

"Tell me what you have planned!" she begged. "It sounds very exciting!"

"I think it will be."

The Marquis thought for a moment before he went on:

"I am fed up with Monte Carlo and I went to the Greek Islands last year, and found them disappointing."

"That was because I was not with you!" Lady Bettine said softly.

"What we will do," the Marquis went on as if she had not spoken, "is to steam through the Suez Canal which I have always wanted to see, down the Red Sea and into the Persian Gulf."

Lady Bettine was silent. She had not the slightest idea where the Persian Gulf was.

Her silence told the Marquis the truth, and he explained:

"It is where the best and finest pearls come from, as they have done for thousands of years!"

"And we can really go there?" Lady Bettine asked.

"We *will* go there," the Marquis promised, "and you can choose the largest pearls you can find to have made into a necklace which will undoubtedly be the envy of all your friends!"

Now Lady Bettine gave a cry of delight that was genuine.

"Oh, darling Selwyn! I cannot imagine anything more exciting, not only to find the pearls, but because we will be together!"

There was a cynical note in the Marquis's voice as he added, as an afterthought:

"We shall be together but, of course, I shall have a party!"

"I suppose so," Lady Bettine conceded, "but I hope no one will interfere, darling, or make it difficult for us."

"I will make sure of that," the Marquis said. "And now, suppose you thank me for an invitation which is at least a

33

little different from what you usually receive."

He pulled Lady Bettine somewhat roughly into his arms.

He kissed her and, as he felt the fire burning on her lips, he thought he would find the trip amusing as well as interesting.

* * *

Driving back to Hawk House two hours later, the Marquis was not thinking of Lady Bettine.

He was intent on his visit to Bahrain.

It had come to him like an inspiration, he thought, when she had disparaged the brooch he had bought for her, and wanted the pearls to be larger.

He had always been interested in jewels, and he was thinking now how pearls were the oldest and the most universal of gems.

The Marquis was a very intelligent man and he had for years studied everything that interested him.

This would have undoubtedly, if they had known of it, astounded his friends.

The Curators of the British Museum, the Wallace Collection and Buckingham Palace would have told a very different story.

The Marquis, when he inherited, appreciated the pictures and furniture his ancestors had collected in all his various Houses.

He had taken the trouble to study them and learn about them.

It had started with pictures and he had delighted the Curator of Buckingham Palace who said ruefully:

"I believe, My Lord, that you know more about the treasures purchased by George IV than I know myself!"

The Marquis, who had heard the same remark from the Curator of the Royal Pavilion at Brighton, had only smiled.

He told himself now it was surprising he had not thought of visiting Bahrain until this moment.

He thought, as he drove on, that pearls had been the

indicator of wealth in the Bible, the Talmud and the Koran.

He was almost certain he was correct in remembering that, before 3,500 B.C., when American Indians and European tribesmen were huddling in caves, civilised Asian Societies looked on pearls as valuable possessions.

Cynically he recalled that to them pearls were a symbol of purity, chastity and innocence, which certainly did not apply to Bettine.

He drove on up Park Lane, thinking of the pearls which were at the moment in the Royal Collections of India, Persia, Egypt, and of course England.

Because it was something new, and something he had not concentrated on before, he felt an undoubted feeling of excitement.

It was the same feeling he had when he saw a new and beautiful face.

When his horse came first past the Winning-Post, and when he brought down to right and left birds that were out of shot to another gun.

"Bahrain!" he said to himself, and it seemed to have a magic sound.

He walked into Hawk House.

He sent for his Secretary to put the wheels in motion which would carry him there as quickly as possible.

* * *

Norita had returned home to pack her trunks.

She had told the Cosnets that they would receive ten shillings per week for as long as they were prepared to look after the house for her.

She could see not only the delight in their eyes but also the relief that they could stay.

"You knows, Miss, we'll keep everythin' nice and proper, just like it were in your dear mother's day," Mrs. Cosnet said. "God rest her soul!"

"I am sure you will," Norita smiled, "and I will give you

35

some money with which to buy chickens, so that if nothing else, you will have eggs."

"We'll be all right, Miss, wi' things in the garden," Mr. Cosnet said, "don't you worry your pretty 'ead about us."

Norita thought it was a blessing that she did not have to worry about them.

She got Cosnet to bring down her trunks from the attic and packed everything she possessed.

It was not much, and she added a few small, but precious, things that had belonged to her mother.

She left behind the books that she and her father had read together which she loved as if they were all friends.

Then she remembered Miss Marsh had said there was a big Library at Hawk Hall.

She thought how exciting it would be to be able to see and use one of the great Libraries she knew were to be found in every ancestral house.

She then went to see the Vicar.

She asked him to keep an eye on the Cosnets and to let her know if they were ill, or if there was anything seriously wrong with the house.

"There is nothing I can do about the leaking roof," she smiled. "It will just have to get worse and worse unless I can make enough money to have it repaired."

"I suppose we can say," the Vicar said with a smile, "that 'what cannot be cured must be endured'!"

They had laughed and he went on:

"Do not worry, my child, I am sure the Cosnets will be all right, and if anything disastrous should happen, everybody in the village, seeing how kind your father and mother always were, will rally round."

That evening Norita had eaten a sparse meal alone in the small Dining-Room.

Then she had gone into the Sitting-Room to say good-bye to things which had been part of her life for eighteen years.

36

It hardly seemed possible that she was to go away from it all.

Instead of being the mistress of her own house, as she had been since her mother died, she was to be merely a servant in someone else's.

"You know it is the only thing I can do, Mama," she said as if her mother was beside her.

She looked round, feeling the tears were not far from her eyes.

"If anything goes wrong," she consoled herself, "I can always come home."

To her surprise, she slept peacefully.

Her small bedroom had once been the Night Nursery and overlooked the garden.

When the first rays of light woke her up she realised it was very cold and the sky was overcast, with the promise of rain later in the day.

She remembered how warm Hawk House had seemed, with a fire burning brightly in the School-Room, piled with coal.

It was not the same as the wood which Cosnet collected every day.

She was also sure the food would be very much more plentiful than the very simple meal she had eaten last night.

"I am very lucky," she told herself, "and what it more, it is an adventure!"

She put on the same clothes she had worn yesterday because they were her best.

Old Cosnet carried her trunks downstairs to where the farmer's son, to whom she had sent a pleading message yesterday, was waiting.

He was sitting on his cart, which smelt of the manure he had carried in it yesterday, but Norita could not afford to be particular.

She said good-bye to Joe Cosnet and to his wife who was tearful at losing her.

37

Then she climbed on to the front of the cart beside Ben Jones.

They set off for the Station.

"Be ye goin' away for long, Miss Norita?" Ben asked.

"I expect so," Norita replied, "and would you ask your father to be very kind and let Joe Cosnet have a few seed potatoes, if he can spare them?"

"Oi'll do that, Miss," Ben said, "an' ye tak care o' yersel'. Oi've heard some strange tales of wot goes on in Lonnon!"

"I hope I shall not be only in London, but in the country," Norita said.

"That be better," Ben said, and added darkly: "Oi don't trust people as lives in big towns."

Norita smiled.

At the same time, she felt a little apprehensive that Miss Marsh did not seem to trust the Marquis.

She was too intelligent not to realise there was something about him which Miss Marsh was keeping to herself.

She guessed that it was because she was so young that the old Governess was not being frank.

"Whatever he does will not worry me," she told herself. "All I have to think about is the Marquis's little daughter."

It worried her however that Lady Alyce should be so limp. She also looked very frail.

After all, the Marquis could afford the very best and most expensive Doctors if there was anything wrong with her.

It did not take long to reach the Station.

It had been far more tiring when she had had to walk there yesterday, then she had walked back again on the return journey.

The old porter greeted her warmly, and took her luggage to the platform.

Norita held out her hand to Ben.

"Good-bye, Ben," she said, "and thank you very much for bringing me here."

"Now ye be careful o' they folks in Lonnon!" Ben warned

as if it was on his mind.

"I will!" Norita promised.

She did not have to wait long for a train.

She purchased her ticket and it was a joy to realise that she could travel First Class without it being on her conscience.

The porter found her a carriage to herself that was marked 'Ladies Only'.

Then she was off!

Norita waved until the Station was out of sight, then she sat down and thought about herself.

"I am going out into the world," she said beneath her breath, "as the village girls do when they take up a position in a Big House where they know no one."

She could understand why the girls, when they were only just fifteen, would cry when they said good-bye to their families.

It was frightening, very frightening.

At the same time she was fortunate in that she was going to a place where Miss Marsh had been for some years.

She knew the people would like and respect her.

However, she thought, it was going to be difficult to behave as a Governess should.

She had always been aware that her father's ancestors were part of the history of England.

Her mother had often said:

"We may be poor, but our blood is as good as anybody's in the country, and it is something, my darling, of which you must always be very proud."

At first Norita had been too young to understand what she meant.

Then she had known that what her mother was saying was that it was not how you lived, it was what you were that mattered.

"There is nothing to be ashamed of in being poor," her father once said to her, "and it is something for which one should not have to apologise."

Norita had often heard him say frankly:

"I cannot afford that."

Or:

"I would help if I had the money."

A lesser man would have prevaricated and made excuses because he was ashamed to admit his poverty.

"I may be in a subservient position," Norita told herself, "but I will not be humble about it, and I will not allow anyone to trample on me!"

She lifted her chin a little at the thought.

At the same time it was frightening to be beholden to someone who paid for her services.

They would therefore expect her to be servile.

Suppose the Marquis ordered her about as if she was a slave?

"My blood is as good as his, and I shall tell him so!"

She spoke the words aloud, then she laughed.

She was letting her imagination run away with her, as it often did.

As Miss Marsh had said, it was unlikely that she would see the Marquis, and even if she did, he was hardly likely to behave like a Roman Emperor.

'And even the slaves revolted!' she thought, remembering her history.

Then she did not wish to think of what had happened to them, in consequence.

* * *

Norita arrived at Paddington Station.

As Miss Marsh had promised, there were two of the Marquis's servants waiting for her on the platform.

She could not fail to recognise their livery with its silver buttons bearing the Marquis's crest.

There was a very smart carriage for her, and a Brake for her trunks.

It was somewhat different from the farm cart in which she

40

had travelled from the village to the Station, and she found herself laughing at the irony of it.

The Marquis's servants, who were obviously very conscious of their position, would be horrified at being expected to travel in a manure-cart!

"As Papa would say, there is nothing wrong in being poor," she told herself, "and 'beggars cannot be choosers!'"

Chapter Three

THE MARQUIS was a perfectionist.

He organised everything he owned with an expertise that was the envy of those who worked for him.

When he started to build his yacht, the *Sea Hawk* he thought, was a nice 'play' on his own name.

He was determined that it would be larger, faster and more luxurious than any other yacht afloat.

He bombarded the ship-builders with alterations and additions, and inspected other people's yachts in various ports of Europe, to make certain his would excel them all.

When finally the *Sea Hawk* was finished, just before Christmas, he was determined to make his first voyage a memorable one.

He had actually not thought of leaving England until later in the year. Now Lady Bettine had, he thought, inspired him to start out as soon as possible.

The idea of visiting the Persian Gulf appealed to him.

It was somewhere he had never been but it had, however, frequently occurred in his mind because he was interested in jewels.

As soon as he arrived back at Hawk House he sat down to choose his party.

He would never have thought of doing anything so unconventional as going alone with any woman, or having too few other guests so that he would find the voyage boring.

With a twist of his lips he was well aware of how quickly the most alluring face and the most passionate body could fail to arouse him.

He therefore sat in his Study going over the names of his innumerable friends, only a few of whom could be described as being close to him.

He chose without any difficulty Lord and Lady Langley.

He had known them for a long time and he had served in the same Regiment as George Langley, although he was an older man.

They were both, he had always thought, his idea of an ideal couple.

They complemented each other, and were so in love, that even after ten years of marriage it would never have crossed Elizabeth's or George's mind to be unfaithful.

Elizabeth Langley had beauty, tact and charm.

She could, as the Marquis knew from the past, soothe ruffled feelings or persuade anybody who was about to be truculent to control themselves.

George, on the other hand, was always good company and able to keep the party laughing.

He was also, and this was important, an excellent Bridge player.

The Marquis, although he was loath to admit it, found even the most beautiful woman was inclined to bore him when he was not making love to her.

He therefore planned that he would have at least three guests who played Bridge as well as he did.

The women could occasionally play a hand, but he would stipulate that, as a general rule, he preferred it to be a male pastime.

This meant he needed two more players, and he hesitated for a moment over Sir Mortimer Garson.

He was an excellent player, but he was also a fairly new acquaintance.

Although he seemed extremely affable, the Marquis was not sure if he really wished to make a close friend of him.

However, the fact that he was so good at Bridge tipped the scales, and he was put down on the list.

This meant that his party would also have to include Lady Hermione Malton.

Hermione Malton was a widow and an outstanding Beauty.

She was very different in looks from Lady Bettine, and the two rivalled each other at being the most acclaimed, both from a public and a private point of view.

People stood on the chairs in Hyde Park to see Lady Bettine go by. Lady Malton's eyes would flash with anger if the same compliment was not accorded to her.

She was certainly very spectacular, and it would be difficult to overlook her, even in the largest crowd.

She had flaming red hair, a magnolia skin and a figure that owed little to tight lacing and was, unlike so many of the Beauties', entirely natural.

For the last two months, Lady Milton had been squired everywhere by Sir Mortimer, and speculation among the gossips was growing as to whether he would succeed her late husband.

If for no other reason than because he was so rich.

That left a place for one more man, and here the Marquis did not hesitate.

His closest friend was The Honourable Peregrine Napier, and was perhaps the only man in whom he ever confided.

'Perry', as he was always called, had been at Eton with him and as he was the same age they had gone on to Oxford together.

After that they had served in the same Regiment and spent a lot of their time exploring the world.

It was unthinkable, the Marquis knew, for him to go abroad without taking Perry with him.

Because he was invariably hard up, Perry spent most of his time with the Marquis and seldom visited his father's gloomy and somewhat dilapidated Castle in Northumberland.

The Marquis was only too willing for Perry to ride his

horses and stay at any of his houses, as long as they could share everything together.

In fact Perry was to the Marquis the brother he had never had.

That completed his party, although he would ask Perry if he wanted to invite any particular woman for his amusement.

He was well aware that Perry was suffering from what he described as 'a dented heart'.

This was because he had lost the Beauty who had enjoyed his company for nearly a year as she had decided to accept an offer of marriage from the Duke of Cumbria.

"You can hardly blame her," Perry had said despairingly to the Marquis, "because as you well know, I have nothing to offer her except myself, and that has very little value in the Marriage Market!"

"I am sorry, old man," the Marquis had said sympathetically, "but there are plenty of other women in the world."

"At the moment," Perry had said angrily, "I have a dislike for the whole damned sex!"

He walked out of the room as he spoke and the Marquis had known there was nothing he could do to comfort him.

He had thought from the very beginning that Sybil Dorchester was only making use of Perry.

She was determined to make a brilliant social marriage which would establish her in Society for the rest of her life.

Perry was besotted with her, which was not surprising. Seeing how beautiful she was, what man in love would listen to reason?

'It will take Perry's mind off Sybil,' the Marquis thought.

He sent a groom to his lodgings to ask him to come to Hawk House immediately.

Then he started to write letters to the rest of the party.

He told them they must leave England in three days' time.

He knew they would all protest that they could not be ready so quickly.

Yet they would all manage it.

Then, having sent for his Secretary, the Marquis started to arrange everything down to the last detail.

As an experienced traveller, he knew it was a mistake to take women through the Bay of Biscay.

He also wanted to have the *Sea Hawk* to himself for the first four days.

'If there is anything wrong that needs altering or needs refitting, we can have it done at Gibraltar,' he thought.

He told his Secretary that he would leave the day after tomorrow.

A private Drawing-Room coach would be attached to the Express at Calais to carry his guests to Marseilles, where he would be waiting for them.

The Marquis completed his instructions as to the servants who would travel on the *Sea Hawk*.

It was only as an afterthought as he was leaving the Study that he said to Mr. Seymour:

"Oh, incidentally, Sir William wishes Lady Alyce to go to the sun. The child and her Governess . . What is her name? — Miss Marsh — can travel with me in the *Sea Hawk*."

Mr. Seymour, who had been jotting down all the orders the Marquis was giving him, raised his head to say that Miss Marsh was leaving.

He was too late. The Marquis had gone.

He told himself that it was immaterial, and what was required was that he should see that Lady Alyce was ready and would, he knew, board the yacht before the Marquis did.

He made a note of it on his pad and hurried away to start his almost Herculean task of having everything ready on time.

The Marquis would have been surprised if he had known the different reactions his invitations received.

Elizabeth and George Langley were at first a little doubtful.

46

"I am perfectly prepared to go anywhere with Selwyn," Lord Langley said, "but I find the women with whom he involves himself incredibly boring after a week in their company."

"I know that, darling," Elizabeth Langley replied, "but when Selwyn has finished with them they cry on my shoulder, and you have a convenient engagement elsewhere!"

She laughed as she spoke and her husband put his arm round her and said:

"I cannot understand why Selwyn cannot find somebody like you. Although I have been married to you for ten years, I feel as if time has stood still, and it is little more than ten months!"

Elizabeth Langley laughed.

"You cannot have said anything that makes me feel happier!"

"The truth is," Lord Langley said, "the more I see of other women, the more I love you!"

His wife kissed him.

"The trouble with you is that, like Selwyn, you are too clever," she said, "and you both expect too much."

"All I ask," Lord Langley said as if he was following his own train of thought, "if we go on this voyage, which I feel will be good for you, is that you protect me from women who whine when Selwyn neglects them and men who try to borrow money because they have lost so much at cards."

His wife laughed.

"I promise to do that, and it really would be a joy to be in the sunshine. You know as well as I do that February is a horrible month in England."

In another house in Mayfair, Lady Malton was staring at the Marquis's invitation as if she could not believe her eyes.

She had made up her mind a few months ago that of all the men she had met, the Marquis was unique.

He was the most attractive, the most outstanding and

47

definitely the most exciting.

Lord Malton had been killed in a hunting accident four years after they had been married.

Their marriage had become undoubtedly acrimonious in the last two years before his death. She had therefore not pretended to mourn a man she had begun to dislike.

Dominating, aggressive, Lord Malton paid little attention to his wife but made a scene if any other man attempted to do so.

Hermione Malton was well aware that she was beautiful.

Her beauty was an obvious attraction to the opposite sex and her parents had been thankful to marry her off almost as soon as she emerged from her School-Room.

Colonel Brent came from a respected County family.

He had been in the Grenadier Guards and was in every way what was called a 'Perfect English Gentleman'.

His wife was equally qualified, but that did not entitle them to be involved with the smart Society who appreciated their daughter's looks and personality.

To their County neighbours, Hermione looked theatrical.

The mothers of the ladylike girls shook their heads and murmured that they would not be surprised if she came to a bad end.

It was easy to see their chagrin when Hermione, at just eighteen, was married to Lord Malton and became part of the pleasure-loving Society which circled round the Prince of Wales.

To Hermione it was like entering Fairyland.

The only snag was that by no stretch of the imagination could she see her husband as 'Prince Charming'.

When he was conveniently removed to another world, she had enough money to entertain and be entertained.

She was, however, sensible enough to realise that at twenty-six she was at the height of her beauty, and it was important that she should find herself the right husband.

Women who looked like her were always suspect.

She was aware that some of the important hostesses sent her invitations occasionally instead of regularly.

She had fixed her mind, her thoughts and her wishes on the Marquis. She wondered how she could entice him away from Lady Bettine.

Now, out of the blue, had come his invitation which was too wonderful an opportunity to be missed.

She had only had the off-chance of talking to the Marquis at dinner or dancing with him at a Ball.

Now she would be with him on his yacht.

She would be one of his guests for at least a month, and she was determined he would not escape.

A little later in the day, Sir Mortimer told her that he was also in the party.

She was not surprised. It was obvious to Hermione Malton that the Marquis was linking them together.

Just as he would have invited Lady Bettine for his own amusement.

"There will be plenty of time to change all that," Hermione Malton said confidently.

She told Sir Mortimer how delightful it was that they would be together on what would be a voyage to Paradise.

Hermione's mind was already fixed on the Marquis.

Very perceptive, she was concerned with signs and portents, lucky charms and witch's spells.

She had little time to think of what to wear on this special voyage as she drove in her smart Brougham, out to Islington.

There she consulted her favourite fortune-teller.

He was an old man who looked as if he was a wizard, and he definitely was more clairvoyant than most soothsayers.

At the same time, as a fashionable teller of fortunes, he made it his business to know a great deal about his clients.

He was careful to keep abreast of the social gossip about them.

Hermione Malton told him she was going on a very

special journey and wished to know what he could see of it in his crystal ball.

It did not take him long to ascertain that she would travel in a yacht.

The *Sea Hawk* had been extolled in all the social magazines as being the finest private ship afloat.

Not a day went by when the Marquis's name was not mentioned in the Social Columns of the newspapers.

To link Lady Malton with the owner of the *Sea Hawk* was not difficult.

He peered into the large crystal ball lying on black velvet. He was silent for a long time before he said:

"I see you are going to the sun, not for a short period, but for a long time. I see dark-skinned men wearing turbans, and porpoises frolicking about in a blue sea."

"Yes, yes, you are right!" Lady Malton said eagerly, "and what else?"

"A handsome man, very handsome! He is clever, distinctive. He grows very easily bored with the ordinary and the commonplace."

"That is very true!" Lady Malton cried excitedly.

"There have been many women in his life," the Soothsayer went on, "and there is one now, but I do not think she will last."

He glanced up at his client and saw as he expected a sudden light in her green eyes.

"No, she will not last," he repeated. "Then the man concerned will look around for somebody else."

"And who do you think that will be?"

The soothsayer bent a little lower over his crystal ball.

"It is difficult to be sure," he said, "but I think — I am almost certain — that she is very different from the woman he is involved with at present."

Hermione gave a deep sigh of relief.

"And her hair?" she asked. "What colour is her hair?"

The soothsayer was silent before he said:

"She is different in many ways, more beautiful, definitely more slender, and I think her hair is like the flames of a fire."

He saw the triumph in the smile on Hermione's lips. Then to make sure she had her money's worth, he added:

"It will not be easy. There will be difficulties and you must beware of a woman. She appears to be your friend, but she is your enemy. Do not trust her!"

"I shall certainly not do that!" Lady Malton said sharply.

He put his hand up to his forehead.

"I can see no more. Perhaps you could come back again another day?"

"You may be sure that I will return."

Hermione put three sovereigns down on the table and rose to her feet.

"I am very grateful to you."

"Beware of other women. They are not lucky for you!"

That was certainly true, Hermione thought as she drove from the rather dingy house.

Women had been jealous and envious of her ever since she could remember, and Lady Bettine was no exception.

But she would defeat her in the end — Hermione Malton was sure of that.

*　*　*

Norita arrived at Hawk House and was shown up to the School-Room.

She found to her surprise that Lady Alyce was sitting in front of the fire with a doll in her lap.

Instead of Miss Marsh there was a housemaid beside her on a chair reading, extremely badly, a Nursery Rhyme.

As the footman showed her in, the young housemaid sprang to her feet saying:

"Oh, 'ere you are, Miss! I was to tell Mrs. Winter as soon as you arrived!"

She hurried out of the room before Norita could speak. Norita walked to the fireplace to say:

"Hello, Alyce! Where is Miss Marsh?"

"She has gone," Alyce said in a dull, expressionless voice.

"Gone?" Norita exclaimed.

Before she could ask another question a woman, whom she saw at a glance was the Housekeeper, came into the room.

"Good-morning, Miss Combe!" she said. "I'm Mrs. Winter and I'm afraid I've some bad news for you."

"Alyce has just told me, Mrs. Winter, that Miss Marsh has gone," Norita said.

"That's true, Miss, she's left you a note which I've here with me, and told me to say how sorry she was."

"I suppose her sister is worse!"

"Much worse, Miss Marsh told me, and there was nothing she could do but leave for Devonshire immediately!"

Norita felt her spirits drop. She had been so certain that Marshy would be there to show her what to do.

She felt suddenly helpless.

"Now, don't you worry," Mrs. Winter said. "Miss Marsh made me promise I'd do everything I could to help you, and I've never been one to break a promise."

"Thank you."

"Now first of all I must tell you," Mrs. Winter went on, "they'll be bringing your trunks upstairs, but they're not to be unpacked."

"Are we going to the country?" Norita asked.

She thought if only that was so it would make things so much easier.

She would be able to cope if she could play with the child in the gardens, ride the horses and enjoy what was to her so familiar.

"What you're doing, Miss Combe," Mrs. Winter was saying, "is leaving in His Lordship's yacht for the sun!"

Norita stared at her almost open-mouthed.

"In His . . Lordship's . . yacht?" she repeated.

"Yes, Sir William Smithson who, as I am sure you know,

52

is the Royal Physician to Her Majesty the Queen, has told His Lordship that Her Ladyship shouldn't stay in this cold, wet climate, so you're boarding the *Sea Hawk* tomorrow morning."

Norita drew in her breath.

For a moment she thought she could not be hearing right.

If it was true, it was the most exciting thing that had ever happened.

When she learnt they were going to Bahrain she was sure she was dreaming.

Later, after luncheon when Alyce lay down to rest, Mrs. Winter told her exactly what Sir William had said.

"The poor child's anaemic, and she also needs a change of interests. If you asks me, it's to be with younger people, which of course is what you are."

She looked at Norita a little critically.

"But I should have thought," she went on, "if you'll forgive me saying so, that you're really too young to be a Governess."

"I am certainly younger than Miss Marsh," Norita said, as she knew by now Marshy must be over sixty.

"What I've thought for years," Mrs. Winter continued, "is that Lady Alyce should be taken out of herself, so to speak. I believe Miss Marsh did suggest that she should have other children to play with, but they're seldom in London, and it's not easy to arrange in the country."

"I can understand that," Norita said, "but I am sure the sunshine will do Lady Alyce good."

"At the end of the day," she added, "it's 'the right food'!"

When her mother had been alive she had made sure that everything they ate was appetising.

Lady Wyncombe had not only cooked herself, but had taught a series of village girls to cook in the same way.

After her mother's death, Norita had done the same and she was an excellent cook.

She had also, as her mother had done, studied the value of different foods.

Mrs. Cosnet had never been a cook, but only a house-maid.

When she was alone, Norita ate what she provided, simply because it seemed too much trouble to cook for herself.

She had therefore looked forward to having again the delicious meals she had enjoyed for so many years.

She was sure that the Marquis would have the same kind of food which her father had always enjoyed.

She was surprised and disappointed when what was served to Alyce and herself at luncheon by two footmen was what she knew the moment she saw it was 'School-Room food'.

There was lamb, which was well-cooked, but very dull.

Boiled potatoes, Brussels sprouts, and cabbage with nothing to commend it except that it was merely edible.

Afterwards there was the typical Nursery fare of rice pudding and stewed plums which had been bottled the previous season.

There was no cream, and the meal finished with Stilton cheese.

While Norita appreciated it she was not surprised that Alyce refused to take any.

The child had picked at the lamb and ate practically nothing, complaining petulantly that she disliked rice pudding.

There was no point in saying anything to the footmen who were only serving the meal.

Norita thought that sooner or later she would have to speak to the Chef.

There was, however, no point in doing so now if they were going away tomorrow.

Tea was again what she might have expected, with thick

sandwiches and a madeira cake, which she had always disliked as a child.

Her own supper was little better.

Alyce was provided with bread-and-milk, and also a large glass of warm milk.

"I hate milk!" she said.

Realising how little the child had eaten all day, Norita knew she must do something, although she was afraid of causing trouble as soon as she arrived. She asked the footman if there was any chocolate in the kitchen.

He looked surprised, but replied:

"I expect Chef 'as some, Miss."

"Then ask him if he would be very kind and mix chocolate with the milk and heat it up again for Her Ladyship."

It was a quarter-of-an-hour before it came upstairs and when it did, Norita persuaded Alyce to drink a little.

"I like that!" she exclaimed, and drank the whole glassful.

A housemaid helped Alyce to have her bath and only left when she was in her nightgown.

Norita put her into bed, saying as she did so:

"Do you say your prayers?"

"When I am not too tired," Lady Alyce answered, "and then Miss Marsh used to say them for me."

"As I want you to go to sleep quickly tonight, because we have such an adventurous day tomorrow," Norita said, "I will say them for you."

She said those she herself had been taught as a child.

Then she added a prayer that her mother had taught her when she was about Alyce's age.

> "Four angels round my bed,
> Two at the bottom, two at the head,
> Two to listen while I pray,
> Two to carry my sins away."

"I like that," Alyce said.

"I will teach it to you tomorrow," Norita said. "It has a special magic for sending you to sleep quickly, and you will wake up feeling well and excited."

"Will you tell me a story about it?" Alyce asked.

"I will tell you a story about that, and where we are going."

Norita had told her several stories during the afternoon, but she began to think of herself and her clothes.

When she had turned out the light in Alyce's room she went into the School-Room to find Mrs. Winter waiting for her.

"That poor child," Mrs. Winter said sitting down heavily at the fireside. "My heart bleeds for her."

"Why?" Norita enquired.

"Because she doesn't seem to enjoy anything," Mrs. Winter said. "Think of it — she has everything a little girl could ever want, and yet half the time she seems to be half asleep."

With difficulty Norita prevented herself from saying that she was sure the child was underfed.

She was quite certain that no one would believe her, but she remembered her mother saying:

"People are happy when they are well-fed. That is why it is better to go without clothes than without food."

Norita remembered how upset her mother had been to find some children in the village who were half-starved.

Their mother was too slatternly to provide them with a proper meal while their father was out of work.

This meant they stole and were always in trouble.

Whenever anybody was ill, her mother would make her beef broth and take it to them to make sure that they drank it.

"Of course, what Her Ladyship wants is a mother," Mrs. Winter was saying, "and to be honest with you, Miss Combe, His Lordship sees very little of her."

"What happened to her mother?" Norita enquired.

"Didn't Miss Marsh tell you?" the Housekeeper asked. "Very sad, it was. Her Ladyship died giving birth."

"That was tragic!" Norita agreed. "Was His Lordship very upset?"

Mrs. Winter hesitated and looked a little uncomfortable.

"I shouldn't be gossiping like this," she said, "but it's best you know the truth."

"That is what I would like to know," Norita replied.

"Well, His Lordship was very young, and so was Her Ladyship, and t'was arranged between their fathers. They didn't have a chance to know each other before they were rushed up the aisle."

"Naturally they were unhappy," Norita said sympathetically.

Mrs. Winter nodded.

"They didn't have the same interests, and I've often thought it was fate that Her Ladyship should have been taken from us."

"So Alyce has lacked a mother's love," Norita said as if to herself.

"She's had nurse after nurse," Mrs. Winter replied, "but she didn't seem to care for any of them. I thought Miss Marsh made her happier than any of the Governesses she had before."

Norita could understand why the Dowager Marchioness had been so insistent that Marshy should look after her grandchild.

"Now, I'm sure, Miss Combe," Mrs. Winter went on, "that you'll do your best for the poor child. She doesn't seem to have much life in her, if you know what I mean."

"I know exactly what you mean!" Norita said.

Then she asked:

"Does His Lordship have a Secretary who sees to the wages?"

"That's Mr. Seymour, but he's very busy at the moment. I

doubt if he'll have time to see you, Miss Combe, before you leave."

Norita thought for a moment before she said:

"Perhaps I could send him a note. It's only that I want part of my wages paid to an old couple who were pensioned off by my father and mother."

"I understand, Miss," Mrs. Winter said, "and if you tell him what it is you want, I'll see he gets it first thing in the morning."

"That would be very kind of you," Norita said, "and I was going to ask if I could possibly have some of my wages in advance as I had some bills to pay before I left home."

That was true. She had also given the Cosnets all the money that was left over from her ticket to London.

Mrs. Winter considered for a moment, then she said:

"I tell you what I'll do, Miss. I'll slip down and see Mr. Seymour myself. I know I can have a word with him when he might be too busy to see you."

"I should be most grateful," Norita said.

She looked rather helpless as she added:

"I have with me everything that I possess, but I am afraid my summer gowns are very shabby."

"There, now," Mrs. Winter exclaimed. "It's just like a man, never thinking when they're going from one place to another in the world that a woman wants clothes!"

Because it sounded so funny, Norita laughed.

"That is undoubtedly true, and I was thinking if we stopped anywhere on the way, I might be able to buy some thinner material to make myself perhaps two cooler dresses."

Mrs. Winter thought for a moment, then she said:

"I'll go and see Mr. Seymour."

Norita quickly wrote a note asking if he would be kind enough to send the Cosnets either ten shillings every week, or a month's money, and deduct it from her salary.

She was afraid that he might forget, in which case the

Cosnets would be in a terrible plight.

She therefore added:

> "*As these two old people are entirely*
> *dependent on what they receive from me,*
> *I would be very, very grateful if you*
> *would make certain they do not go for*
> *any length of time without some money.*"

She signed her name and only hoped that Mr. Seymour would not think she was being difficult in making extra work for him the minute she arrived.

Taking the note, Mrs. Winter went down the stairs.

She was away for such a long time that Norita, who wanted to go to bed, was afraid she had forgotten.

She had already been told that she and Alyce were to have breakfast at eight-thirty, and leave the house an hour later.

Then at last Mrs. Winter returned.

"I've seen Mr. Seymour, Miss," she said, "and he's promised your people'll have their money sent the first of every month."

"Thank you very much," Norita replied.

"Why I've been so long," Mrs. Winter went on, "I was looking out this material, which I was sure I had somewhere. It's muslin which you can make into very pretty dresses when the weather gets warmer."

She produced some muslin which Norita suspected had been bought for curtaining.

It was very fine, and expensive, and there was one roll in white and another with little blue flowers, which she thought was lovely.

"I've had it for years, Miss," Mrs. Winter said as she thanked her, "and I'm sure it'll make several gowns that can easily be washed."

"I am sure they will," Norita said, "and thank you, very, very much!"

She packed the two rolls of material in her trunk that was in her bedroom, and having put on her nightgown, she got into bed.

It was then that the excitement of where they were going seeped over her.

She felt as if her father was telling her how exciting it would be to sail up the Persian Gulf and visit Bahrain.

She had talked about it to her father because the name 'Norita' was Greek for Pearl.

He had said that pearls would mean something special to her as she was named after them.

'I wish I had known where we were going before I left home,' she thought. 'I am sure there must be something about Bahrain among his books.'

For a moment she felt almost angry that it had all happened so quickly.

Then she thought that the Marquis might not be a reader.

Yet she would have the opportunity if they stopped at Marseilles, or perhaps Alexandria, to find some guide-books.

She was still thinking about it the next morning when a footman brought her a note on a silver salver.

"From Mr. Seymour, Miss."

Norita opened it and found with delight it contained her first month's wages.

He had deducted what he had sent to the Cosnets.

For a moment it seemed such a lot of money that she felt there must be a mistake.

Then she told herself with delight that now she would buy lots of books as, thanks to Mrs. Winter, she need not spend anything on clothes.

"No one will look at me anyway," she told her reflection in the mirror."

Breakfast was exactly what she had expected: a thick, heavy porridge, eggs, bacon and toast that was cold before it arrived upstairs.

She was not surprised that Alyce ate very little.

Fortunately, somebody in the kitchen had had the intelligence to put chocolate into her milk.

She drank that.

Then, as it was very cold outside, Alyce was dressed in a very pretty coat of white ermine with the same fur trimming her bonnet.

She also had a pair of leggings to keep her feet warm.

Norita had the same, slightly old-fashioned coat she had worn before.

Her plain felt hat was the one in which she had travelled.

She thought the servants who saw her into the small carriage looked at her disdainfully, but she might just have been imagining it.

There were four horses to draw them, and only just before they set off did Norita ask:

"Are we going by train?"

"Oh, no, Miss," the Butler replied. "I thought Mr. Seymour would 'ave told you — you're boarding His Lordship's yacht at Greenwich."

Norita looked surprised.

At the same time, she thought she might have guessed that the Marquis would have made everything easy for himself.

In the previous century, anyone wishing to cross the Channel had first to make the long drive to one of the Coastal Ports.

Today it was a train journey, but one which inevitably took a long time.

Now Alyce and she had only to drive to Greenwich, then they would be aboard the *Sea Hawk*.

She pressed Mrs. Winter to tell her about it.

But the Housekeeper could tell her little more than she had read in a magazine.

It was not something she could afford to buy, but the Vicar's wife took one regularly and lent it to Norita when she had finished with it.

The yacht had been described, she remembered, as being the largest afloat with the exception of the *Britannia*.

She had been interested simply because her father had several books on ships, and they had studied them together.

Alyce leant back limply against the well-cushioned carriage.

There was a foot-warmer for their feet and they were both covered by a sable-trimmed rug which Norita thought was the height of luxury.

After they had driven for a little way, Alyce asked:

"Will you tell me a story?"

"Yes, of course," Norita replied, "but if I tell you a story I want you to tell me one. It is only fair."

"How can I tell you a story?" Alyce enquired.

"You can tell me about a little girl who went in a big ship to find the most Perfect Pearl in the world!"

"Is that me?"

"I think you can guess that it is."

"And what does a Perfect Pearl look like?"

"That," Norita replied, "is what we are going to find out, and I think it will be very, very exciting!"

Alyce thought this over for a little while before she said:

"What will we do with the Pearl when we find it?"

"It will be a Magic Pearl," Norita said, "and when you hold it in your hand you can wish and your wish will come true."

For the first time the child seemed almost interested.

Then after a little while she relapsed into silence, and Norita was certain it was because she was tired.

'I am sure neither the doctors nor the Marquis realise that she is not eating enough to keep a mouse alive', she told herself.

By the time they reached Greenwich, which was in a little over two hours, she had made up her mind.

Whatever anyone might think or say, and that included the Marquis, she would make Alyce into a normal child.

They drove down to the Quayside, then when Norita saw the *Sea Hawk* she drew in her breath from sheer astonishment.

It was absolutely enormous! It was also exceedingly elegant and undeniably romantic.

It was a ship that seemed, Norita felt, as if it had come out of her dreams, and she could hardly believe she was really going to be a passenger on it.

"Look, Alyce!" she exclaimed, "just look at your Father's marvellous, exciting yacht!"

Alyce opened her eyes, but she did not seem very interested.

"It is going to carry us a long way across the world," Norita went on, " to find the Perfect Pearl."

Alyce did not reply.

Norita wished she had somebody with her who was as excited as she was herself about the voyage.

When they were taken on board, the Captain welcomed them and put them in the charge of a middle-aged man who was, Norita learned, the Chief Steward.

"I'm Johnson, Miss," he said, "and I 'opes you and 'er Ladyship will enjoy the voyage."

"I am sure we shall," Norita smiled.

"I 'spects you'd like to see your cabins, then I'll show you, if you're not too tired, round the yacht."

"We would love that."

He took them below and Norita was astonished at how large the yacht was.

It was new and Johnson obviously wished to show off. He took them into the Marquis's cabin which filled the whole front of the bow.

It was luxuriously furnished and, opening out of it, Norita was shown proudly that there was a bathroom.

Next to that was the Marquis's private Study, and here Norita gave an exclamation of joy, for the whole of one wall was covered with books!

She thought it might be difficult to get hold of them, but she was determined to try.

The other cabins were all beautifully furnished with the furniture fitting into the walls.

There was a profusion of mirrors which would please any woman, and cupboards fitted with special places for shoes.

The insides were lit with electric light, which Norita had never seen in a wardrobe before.

There was room for at least twenty guests in the main part of the ship.

She found that she and Alyce were as far away from the Marquis's guests as possible.

"Obviously," she told herself, "separating the sheep from the goats."

It would have been impossible however for her to find fault with the very comfortable cabins allotted to them.

There was a Sitting-Room which Johnson told her had originally been intended as the Sick Room.

"I 'opes it won't happen on this voyage," he said, "but I've had instructions from His Lordship to fix it up with everything Her Ladyship might need."

There was a comfortable sofa, two arm-chairs, and a table at which they could work, as well as have their meals.

There were also some bookcases containing a number of children's books.

"I am sure you have thought of everything," Norita said.

"Now all you've got to do, Miss, is to ask me if there's anythin' you wants," Johnson said, "an' I'll see yer gets it."

"You could not be kinder," Norita smiled.

Then she said a little tentatively:

"What I would like to do is to see the Galley, and if it is possible, to have a word with the Chef."

"O' course!" Johnson replied. "Come along then. 'E'll be there now preparing Luncheon."

He took them to the Galley.

Norita had never seen one before, but she was sure it was an exceptional example of its kind.

Everything was gleaming white and she could see a number of cooking gadgets which she knew would have delighted her mother.

There was a man dressed in a Chef's tall white hat cutting up some meat and, as Norita looked at him, her heart leapt.

He was French.

"*Monsieur*," the Steward said, mispronouncing the word, "here's a lady wishes to meet you. Miss Combe's the Governess to Her Ladyship."

"*Enchanté, Mademoiselle!*" the Chef said.

"*Bon jour, Monsieur*," Norita replied in her excellent French. "I am delighted to meet you, and I have a great favour to ask."

The Frenchman looked at her in astonishment.

"*Vous parlez français, Mademoiselle?*"

"*Oui, bien sûr.* I hope you can understand me," Norita answered with a smile.

She then started to talk almost as quickly as he did, explaining that Lady Alyce was suffering from anaemia, and she felt certain, she told him, it was due to wrong feeding.

"It is not bad food, *Monsieur*," she went on to explain, "but you as a Frenchman will understand that it is very, very dull, and therefore Her Ladyship will not eat it."

The Chef threw his hands up in a typically French gesture.

He said something, almost beneath his breath, derogatory about English cooking and the English *appétit*.

"What I was going to ask you, if I had the opportunity," Norita went on, "is if you could arrange to give Lady Alyce some liver almost every day, and only you, *Monsieur*, could make it so palatable that she will enjoy it."

She saw her flattery was taking effect and told him how her mother had made beef teas from the best beef for people who were ill.

They were talking animatedly 'nineteen to the dozen',

while Johnson and the Assistant Chef listened in astonishment.

Finally the Chef said:

"I'll make a little wager with you, *Mademoiselle*, that in one week, Milady'll be a different child. In two weeks a happy one, and in three everybody'll say she's a nuisance and they can't cope with her, she's so wild!"

Norita laughed and held out her hand.

"It is a bet, *Monsieur*, but I feel it is one you will win!"

When Alyce had been tempted with some sugared cherries, they went back to their cabins.

As they did so, Norita felt she had won a great victory.

She told herself if it did not please the Marquis when he saw the difference in his little daughter, nothing would.

Chapter Four

THE MARQUIS arrived at Greenwich far later than he had intended.

He had gone to say goodbye to Lady Bettine and had found her reclining elegantly in her *Boudoir*.

What was meant to be just a few words of love developed into something far more passionate.

It was two hours before the Marquis was once again on his way.

Already his mind had turned to his plans for the voyage.

He was checking over the new gadgets which had been installed since his last visit to the *Sea Hawk*.

He thought he would be very angry if they were not working as efficiently as he expected.

It was dark when he arrived at Greenwich and drove down to the Quay.

The Captain was waiting to welcome him aboard and, as soon as he had done so, the gang-plank was pulled in.

The Marquis gave the order for them to put to sea.

He went up on the Bridge and watched the ship leave. When it was moving swiftly down river on the evening tide he went to his cabin to change for dinner.

As he might have expected, as it was his first night aboard, his Chef excelled himself.

The Marquis enjoyed some new dishes he had not tasted previously.

When he had finished, despite the cold, he went to the Bridge.

He stayed there until the *Sea Hawk* had reached the English Channel.

He had no intention of dropping anchor at night in some quiet bay, as they would do after they had picked up his guests.

He thought it would be good for the crew and for the yacht to keep steaming on until they reached Marseilles.

He was in fact very pleased with the way the *Sea Hawk* was moving. He did not go below until he was actually feeling sleepy.

This was partly due to Lady Bettine.

Also, he had stayed awake the previous night thinking of the voyage to Bahrain.

He was checking his plans in his mind and making sure he had forgotten nothing in his preparations for the voyage.

When the Marquis awoke the following morning, the weather had worsened and the sea was rough.

As soon as he had finished breakfast, the Marquis was once again on the Bridge where he stayed for most of the day.

It was only when it was growing dark that he suddenly remembered that his daughter was aboard and he had not given her a single thought until now.

He was sure everything had been done for her comfort.

He remembered when he had arrived that the Captain had said that Lady Alyce and her Governess were already accommodated in their cabins.

As the Marquis thought of Alyce he was aware that the yacht was rolling quite considerably.

Occasionally it was pitching and tossing.

He hoped the child was a good sailor, but as he had never taken her to sea before he did not know the answer one way or another.

'I suppose I ought to go and find out for myself,' he thought.

He walked along the passage which led to the cabins he

had decided were most suitable for the child, although she was, fortunately, always very quiet.

He had no wish to have his guests disturbed unnecessarily.

As he reached the cabin and opened the door, he recalled he had given orders it should be changed from a sleeping apartment into a Sitting-Room.

For a moment he thought it was empty.

Then he saw there were two people lying on the floor. One was his daughter and the other was obviously her Governess.

He thought it was a strange position for Miss Marsh, who had always seemed very dignified.

Then he saw that Alyce was drawing on a sheet of white paper and her Governess was doing the same thing.

"I have finished my Pearl, Miss Combe," Alyce was saying. "I have made it very, very big. It would be difficult for her to drink it quickly!"

"And I have nearly finished my Fighting Merman," a soft voice answered, "then we will see who wins the prize."

"I suppose that is what you are expecting me to give you," the Marquis remarked.

Two faces looked up at him.

To his astonishment, he saw the woman he had thought to be Miss Marsh had very large eyes in a small, heart-shaped face.

Her hair was fair, and so pale it seemed almost silver in the light from the lamp.

She appeared so young that it flashed through the Marquis's mind that Alyce had brought a friend aboard the yacht.

Then his daughter scrambled to her feet and went towards him saying:

"Look, Papa! I have drawn Cleopatra's ear-ring, the one she did not drink, and it must have been a very, very big Pearl!"

The Marquis took the piece of paper from Alyce. As the ship was rolling uncomfortably, he sat down in the nearest chair.

As he did so, Norita managed to stand up by holding on to a table.

One glance at her told the Marquis she was not the child he had expected her to be.

She was very slender and her gown had obviously been worn a great number of times, but it showed the curves of her figure and revealed the smallness of her waist.

"Who are you?" he asked abruptly.

"I am the new Governess, My Lord. I expect you have been told that Miss Marsh had to leave suddenly."

"I was told nothing!" the Marquis replied.

The ship rolled.

Norita held frantically to the table to prevent herself from staggering.

"You had best sit down," he said, "and tell me what is happening."

There was a sharp note in his voice because, if there was one thing he disliked, it was surprises.

He thought it extremely remiss of Seymour not to have informed him that there was a new Governess, and certainly as she seemed much too young for the position.

"You have not looked at my Pearl!" Lady Alyce said, holding onto the arm of her father's chair.

"I am looking at it now," the Marquis said, "and I consider it a very good effort, but you will see lots of pearls which you can draw in Bahrain."

"That is what Miss Combe said, and she says they are the most precious jewels in the world!'

"I suppose this is a history lesson," the Marquis said, looking across the table at Norita.

"It is the easiest and undoubtedly the most delightful way, My Lord, of learning history," she replied.

He noticed she had a dimple at the corner of her mouth.

"Perhaps you would explain to me who you are and what experience you have had," the Marquis suggested.

"My name is Norita Combe."

The Marquis thought for a moment. Then he said:

"So that is why you are interested in pearls!"

He thought the surprise in Norita's eyes was insulting.

"Are you really aware that 'Norita' is Greek for a pearl?" she asked.

"I am not entirely an ignoramus!" the Marquis retorted.

"I . . I am sorry, perhaps that is something I should . . not have said!" Norita replied, "but I think you are the only person for years who has not exclaimed: 'What a strange name! I have never heard of it before!'"

The Marquis laughed.

"I was thinking that my Greek is not as fluent as I should like it to be, and as it was when I was at Oxford."

"That is a pity," Norita said. "It is such a help in other languages."

The Marquis was about to express his surprise that she should know any languages but her own.

Then Alyce picked up the piece of paper on which Norita had been drawing and said excitedly:

"Oh, now I see what you mean about the Fighting Merman! And was his whole body really a pearl?"

She moved a little unsteadily to her father's side to show him the drawing.

"Look, Papa! Miss Combe has told me all about the Merman, and he looks very fierce!"

The Marquis looked down at the piece of paper which his daughter was holding.

The beautiful piece of 16th century Baroque jewellery had been surprisingly well drawn.

It was a pendant that was reputed to have come originally from the Roman Empire, where the stupendous Baroque pearl had been found which formed the torso of the Merman.

It was something the Marquis had admired when he had seen pictures of it, and longed to possess it.

It certainly surprised him to see it depicted so cleverly by the young woman sitting opposite him.

"I see you are an artist, Miss Combe," he said dryly.

Norita laughed, and it was a very pretty sound.

"I wish that were true, My Lord, but as several great artists have said: 'I do what I can, not what I would'."

She spoke confidently.

The Marquis, who was used to servants who were either tongue-tied, or else trembling in front of him, was surprised.

"I must commend you, not only on your skill, but also by interesting my daughter in trying to draw, and of course, teaching her the history of Cleopatra."

There was a caustic note in his voice as he thought few women could resist thinking and talking of Cleopatra.

He knew that quite a number imagined themselves to be the reincarnation of one of the Great Beauties of the World.

"I have always, ever since I was a child, been fascinated by how she impressed Mark Antony by crushing and drinking one of the most valuable pearls in the world," Norita said, "and it is a story which Alyce has also found enthralling."

"It was a terrible waste, was it not, Papa?" Alyce said.

"It was indeed!" the Marquis agreed, "and I am only hoping when we reach Bahrain you will not want to drink a lot of pearls, which would prove very expensive for me!"

Alyce laughed, and the Marquis thought it was a long time since he had heard his daughter do so.

He was trying to think and take his eyes from Norita.

He was well aware that she was lovely, but in a very different way from anyone he had ever seen before.

There was something about the way her eyes looked at him directly, as well as the faint smile on her lips which made her original.

He then told himself incredulously that she was not admiring him, but although he could hardly believe it, criticising him.

Then he told himself that he was just being imaginative.

If there was anything different about this young woman, it was obviously due to the fact that she was nervous.

"I am wondering, Miss Combe," he said aloud, "if you are a good sailor. I have a feeling we shall be in for a rough passage in the Bay of Biscay."

"That is something I have been wondering myself," Norita replied, "but I promise you Alyce and I will be as little nuisance as possible. If it is very rough, we will stay in bed and read."

She hesitated, then gave him a somewhat questioning glance before she added:

"I am hoping, My Lord, that you will provide us with the necessary books."

It was then that the Marquis was aware that one difference in this very young Governess was that she spoke to him as if he was an equal.

Although it seemed strange, she was definitely not afraid of him.

"I think," he said after a moment, "you will find my books somewhat dull, heavy and definitely above the head of Alyce."

"All I can say is that I have never yet found a book that was dull," Norita said, "and although you have provided us here in the School-Room with a book-case, it is lamentably empty."

That she should make what was a criticism of her surroundings was astounding, and the Marquis considered rebuking her for doing so.

Then he changed his mind.

At least, he thought, this young woman might arouse Alyce from her lethargy. It was something nobody had been able to do before.

He was quite certain, however, when she had seen the books in his private cabin, her interest would fade away.

"You must tell me, Miss Combe," he said, "what are your special interests, and of course, I must do my best to accommodate you."

"Thank you very much," Norita said, "and as Alyce enjoys stories, I am sure they will stimulate my imagination so that I can stimulate hers."

"Miss Combe tells me lovely stories, Papa," Alyce said, "and I am going to have a story about every Port at which we call, and every country we pass!"

"That certainly sounds like an excellent curriculum!" the Marquis said. "I only hope you can keep Miss Combe up to it."

As he spoke, Norita knew that he was thinking she was merely showing off.

With difficulty she resisted an impulse to tell him what she knew about the Mediterranean countries.

They had always interested her, as they had her father.

Instead she told herself that he only liked being with women who talked gossip and were also convinced, as her father had often said, that anything outside England was not worth thinking about.

To the Marquis's astonishment he found he was aware of Norita's thoughts.

He had no idea why this should be so, and thought it must be because her eyes were so large and expressive.

At the same time, so young and innocent.

It passed through his mind that it was the first time for years he had sat talking to an attractive woman without her trying to flirt with him.

"Apart from History, Miss Combe," he said, "what are your particular interests?"

"One, which I think Your Lordship will understand better than any others, is horses."

Norita spoke so sincerely that the Marquis was aware that it was not what he might have thought was 'sucking up' to him because he had such an outstanding stable.

"By that," he remarked, "I presume you have lived in the country."

"Yes, all my life," Norita said, "and as I have had to travel in my mind with, of course, the aid of books, it is very thrilling for me . . to be aboard this magnificent yacht and be able to travel in reality!"

She spoke in a rapt little voice, which told the Marquis how much it meant to her.

He also thought it was a rapture which he usually heard when a woman was talking about him personally.

"I am interested," he said after a slight pause, "in how my Secretary, Mr. Seymour, found you when Miss Marsh, who has been with Alyce for some time, had to leave."

Because the Marquis was easier to talk to than she had expected, Norita told the truth.

"I came to see Miss Marsh to ask her help."

"Why did you do that?"

"Because she taught me for years and she was the one person I thought could assist me to find employment."

"Miss Marsh taught you?" the Marquis asked.

"We lived in the same village," Norita said quickly.

"Now I understand!" the Marquis exclaimed. "So, as Miss Marsh wished to leave she handed over her position to you."

"It was a great relief to me, and I am sure I can look after Alyce nearly as well as Miss Marsh did."

"She tells me lovely stories, Papa," Alyce said again.

She had been looking at her drawing until she heard her name mentioned, and now as she realised that her father was talking about her she said:

"I like Miss Combe, and she does things quicker than Miss Marsh."

"You must tell your father that is what you are going to be — very quick," Norita said, "and it all depends upon how much you eat!"

"I have eaten lots and lots today," Alyce said.

"Yes, you have been very good," Norita answered.

She looked across the table at the Marquis and added:

"I would like, My Lord, when you find it convenient, to have a word with you, if you can spare me the time."

"Of course I can spare the time," the Marquis said. "At what hour does Alyce go to bed?"

"At six o'clock."

"When you can leave her, come to my Private Cabin, which I gather from our conversation you have already inspected."

"Your Chief Steward showed it to us when we arrived," Norita explained. "I was tremendously impressed with the whole yacht!"

"I am glad it pleases you!"

There was definitiely a touch of sarcasm in the Marquis's voice.

He found it hard to believe the conversation he was having with this very young girl. It might easily have been with a Dowager who was condescending to him.

"I have never seen a yacht before," Norita went on, "but I am sure what I have read about the *Sea Hawk* in the newspapers is right, and it is an absolute triumph of British workmanship!"

Again the Marquis looked surprised.

He knew any other woman would have said it was a triumph of his ingenuity.

He rose to his feet, being careful to hold onto the table as he did so.

"I shall see you later, Miss Combe! Goodnight, Alyce!"

He bent down to kiss his daughter perfunctorily on the cheek.

Moving with the experience of a sailor, he reached the

76

door and let himself out.

As soon as he had gone Alyce said:

"Now let us go on drawing — Papa never said who had won the prize!"

"We will draw him another picture tomorrow," Norita promised, "and make sure he gives us a prize after he has seen it."

"He did not say he wanted to frame my picture," Lady Alyce said after a moment.

"I think the best thing we can do is to make a whole collection of drawings, then at the end of the voyage, perhaps we could make them into a book and present them to somebody who will be pleased to have them."

Alyce thought this over. Then she said:

"I think that is a very nice idea. I am sure Granny would like a book."

"I am sure she would," Norita answered.

She thought as she helped Alyce undress that it was not only the food that would take away the child's lethargy.

What she really needed was Love.

She could remember when she was the same age how her father had talked to her, taken her riding, and explained everything she found puzzling.

It had been in a way that made everything he said seem exciting, and very often amusing.

She had never gone to bed without her mother kissing and cuddling her.

She could remember running down the stairs when her mother returned from shopping, or visiting somebody, to throw her arms around her neck and cry excitedly:

"You are back, Mama! You are back! I have missed you!"

She had learned a great deal from Mrs. Winter of the Marquis's indifference towards his daughter, although the Housekeeper had not exactly put it into words.

She had, however, because Mrs. Winter was a gossip,

heard of many women who occupied the Marquis's time.

He paid a great deal more attention to them than he did his daughter.

"And downstairs they're betting," Mrs. Winter said as she sat in front of the School-Room fire, a cup of tea in her hand, "who'll be in His Lordship's party."

She gave a little laugh before she said:

"There's no need to guess or to question whether Lady Bettine Daviot will be there. She's His Lordship's latest, and very beautiful!"

She went on to describe how the public stood on chairs to see Lady Bettine drive by, and how when she appeared in a box at the Theatre she was clapped.

"I wouldn't mind having a small bet with you, Miss Combe," Mrs. Winter went on, "that the whole reason for this sudden rush to the sun has something to do with Lady Bettine! I heard as how His Lordship was away, and it'd be a pity if he came back before she left."

"His Lordship?" Norita asked.

"Lord Daviot, a nice Gentleman! But very much older than his wife."

"Are you . . saying that Lady Bettine . . is married?"

"Oh, yes, dear, she's married! His Lordship never has anything to do with the young girls. Afraid he'd find himself married if he did!"

Norita drew in her breath.

She was very innocent but she knew from the way Mrs. Winter talked that the Marquis was in love with the beautiful Lady Bettine.

It had never struck her for one moment that she would be a married woman.

She was sure her mother would have been extremely shocked at the idea of anybody as important as the Marquis being in love with another man's wife.

"Of course," Mrs. Winter went on, "there have been many ladies breaking their hearts over the Master, and who shall blame them? Seeing how handsome he is!"

"Breaking their . . hearts?" Norita murmured beneath her breath.

"That's only a way of talking," Mrs. Winter replied. "I often think the way they goes on they haven't much heart, and it's all a kind of social game, if you know what I mean."

Norita had no idea, but Mrs. Winter was continuing:

"No one is supposed to get hurt, and no one complain when the fun's over. But you mark my words — it's always the women as suffers, Miss Combe, while the men gets off scot-free!"

"Then . . why do they . . do it?"

Norita was not quite certain exactly what they did do, but it was obviously very disturbing.

"That's a good question, Miss Combe, and if you asks me it's just boredom. They've got nothin' better to do than doll themselves up and hope that some man will be bowled over by their good looks!"

Norita laughed.

"That certainly does seem a waste of time!"

"Then there's letters passing from door to door," Mrs. Winter went on as if she had not spoken, "assignations in secret places, and of course there's always the fear that the lady's 'usband might call His Lordship out."

"Call him out?" Norita queried.

"Fight a duel, my dear! They've been forbidden by Her Majesty and frowned on by all the more respectable people. But of course it happens!"

She sighed and continued:

"Then some poor Gentleman, usually the injured party, I am told, gets his arm in a sling for a month at least."

To Norita it all seemed bewildering.

As Mrs. Winter continued describing how fascinating the Marquis was, and how many women filled his life, she told herself she despised him.

She could understand it if the women had been widows.

But surely he should have some sense of decency and honour not to deceive the husbands of the women he fancied, neglecting his own child in the process.

"He should marry someone suitable," Norita told herself later after Mrs. Winter had left her, "and have a son, which is what Papa would have loved."

Now that she had seen the Marquis she could understand in a way why women found him attractive.

They were prepared to break their marriage vows for him.

At the same time she thought how hard her father had worked, training horses in order to sell them.

How happy he and her mother had been together. She thought the Marquis was obviously very foolish. Surely he must want a son to inherit his title?

Also a number of other children to fill his house with joy and laughter.

Instead of which he had one poor, miserable, neglected little daughter.

There was no use pretending that servants could take the place of a father or a mother, however kind they might be.

Doctors, even one as important as Sir William Smithson, did not understand that Alyce was not eating the right food.

Norita thought of the children in the village whom she had known ever since they were born. They had always been happy and noisy.

The two things went together, and that was what she would make sure that Alyce was.

As she moved along the passage towards the Marquis's cabin, manoeuvring herself skilfully as the ship was rolling, she thought:

'I do not suppose her Father will understand.'

* * *

Norita had heard Alyce's prayers.

She had repeated the one about the four Angels because she liked it.

"Tomorrow," she said as she tucked the child up, "we will go on deck if it is not too rough, and look for the Mermaids riding the white horses."

"In the sea?" Alyce asked.

"Yes, in the sea," Norita promised.

She bent to kiss Alyce who put her arms around her neck.

"Promise you will tell me a story all about them," she pleaded.

"Of course I will," Norita answered, "and perhaps we can find a picture of a Mermaid in the books in your father's cabin."

"That would be lovely!"

Alyce snuggled down against her pillow with a smile on her lips and Norita asked herself why the Marquis could not come and say goodnight to his daughter.

Her father had always come to her.

'At least he has no one else to kiss for the moment!' she thought scornfully.

Then, once again, she remembered Lady Bettine was married and felt herself give a little shudder because it was so unpleasant:

"I want to think about beautiful things," she told herself as she reached the Marquis's cabin door, "and I know when we are in the Mediterranean it will be the most beautiful place I have ever seen!"

She turned the handle and, as the door opened, she saw that the Marquis was waiting for her.

"Come in, Miss Combe," he said, "and I suggest you sit down quickly!"

The ship rolled as he spoke and Norita did as he suggested.

The chair in which she sat was very large and comfortable.

The Marquis thought she looked very sylph-like and insubstantial in it.

He realised she was wearing the same dress she had been wearing an hour ago.

He was experienced where women's clothes were concerned.

It was strange she had made no effort to smarten herself up.

The lights he had arranged in what he thought of as his Study were very bright.

He thought the colour of Norita's hair was not only unusual, but in fact very beautiful.

Her skin was translucent and it suddenly struck him that her name was apt, and she herself was very like a pearl.

"I wanted to speak to you," Norita was saying, "about Alyce."

The Marquis noted that she did not call the child 'Lady' Alyce, as every other Governess had done when speaking to him.

"I am listening to what you have to say," he replied, "but if you are going to tell me she is not interested in anything and very hard to teach, I have heard it all before!"

He paused to add:

"I expect you have already been told that Sir William Smithson thinks she is anaemic."

"She is anaemic," Norita agreed, "and it is because she has not been fed with the right food, and she is limp because she has little in her life to interest her."

If she had thrown a bomb at the Marquis, he could not have been more astonished.

"What do you mean — nothing in her life?" he demanded. "My daughter has everything she could possibly want or require."

"Except for the one thing that is more important than anything else," Norita replied.

'And what is that?"

"It is something quite simply called 'Love'!"

The Marquis stared at Norita as if he could not be hearing right.

Heaven knew, he was used to women talking to him about Love.

But he was not prepared to be taken to task for the lack of it in his daughter's life, certainly not by a young woman who was little more than a Senior Servant.

"You do not know what you are saying," he replied defensively.

"It is natural for children to be loved," Norita said, "and as Alyce has no mother, the only person who can give it to her is of course yourself!"

"Are you inferring that I do not love my daughter?" the Marquis asked sharply. "I. . ."

He stopped because he realised that what he had been about to say was untrue.

He was remembering how often his grandmother and a number of his other relatives had begged him to marry again, not only to provide an heir, but also to give 'poor little Alyce' a mother.

It was inevitable that this tiresome young woman who had just come into his household should say the same thing.

Then, as he did not speak, Norita went on:

"I am sure that Aylce is actually suffering from a form of malnutrition. I therefore spoke to your Chef yesterday evening when we came aboard and today she has eaten a reasonable amount."

She looked at the Marquis defiantly and added:

"I felt this evening there was a little more life in her than there had been for a long time."

"Can you really be saying that my child is being starved?" the Marquis asked angrily.

"Not deliberately," Norita answered, "but the food sent up to the School-Room for luncheon yesterday was so dull and so ordinary that it wouldn't have encouraged anybody to eat! Today it was different, and I am sure what your Chef produces will be surprisingly effective."

83

She gave a little laugh as she added:

"He is quite convinced, as I am, that Alyce will be a different child by the time the voyage comes to an end."

"I see you have everything planned, Miss Combe!" the Marquis said sarcastically.

"That, as I am sure Your Lordship realises, is only one part of the story," Norita answered. "The rest is up to you!"

The Marquis stiffened.

There was just a touch of steel in his grey eyes which made most people recoil from him sharply.

Norita merely said:

"Please try, until your friends arrive, to see a little more of Alyce. Perhaps she could have Luncheon with you, or you could take her with you on the Bridge."

She thought before she added:

"If you showed her the engines, it would be far more exciting than anybody else doing it."

Because now she was pleading with him, the Marquis felt his anger subside.

Norita looked so young, and yet, at the same time, she was speaking earnestly and seriously, as an older woman might have done.

He was also perceptively aware that she was fighting for something which mattered to her.

It was rather touching that she should care so much about a child she hardly knew.

He could not help thinking there must have been a good many men to tell her how lovely she was.

They would also be ready to make sure there was no reason for her to work.

Yet, there was an air of purity and innocence about Norita which he had never encountered before, but which was undeniably there.

Once again she was looking at him critically, and it was a new experience that he found astonishing.

"I will certainly consider what you have said, Miss

Combe," he replied, "and as you say, before my guests arrive, I will be able to concern myself with Alyce without neglecting them."

"Thank you, My Lord. That is what I wished you to say," Norita replied.

She rose from her chair as she spoke.

The Marquis thought with a wry smile that it was usually he who ended the conversation.

"While you are here," he said, "perhaps you would care to choose a book?"

He saw Norita's eyes light up and knew it was something she could not have faked, but was a genuine reaction to his offer.

"I suppose," she said thoughtfully, "you do not have a picture of Mermen and Mermaids in your Library? I have been trying to describe to Alyce what they look like."

"Do you believe in Mermaids, Miss Combe?" the Marquis asked sceptically.

He saw her dimple again before she replied:

"I want to believe in them, My Lord, and they are what Alyce should believe in at her age, and should be part of the enchanted voyage to Bahrain."

The Marquis laughed.

"You are quite right, Miss Combe, and although I cannot promise to find you a picture of a Mermaid here, we will certainly search for one in Gibraltar, and if unsuccessful, in Marseilles."

"That would be lovely!" Norita said. "And please, may I have books, if you have them, on Egypt, Mecca and, of course, Bahrain?"

"Are these for your enjoyment, or Alyce's?" the Marquis enquired.

"Both," Norita answered. "There is so much more I want to learn about all those places and I will tell stories about them to Alyce, which will of course be a History and Geography lesson at the same time!"

Again the Marquis laughed.

Moving to his shelves he found a book on Egypt and another on Arabia.

"I see I have been very remiss," he said, "in not having brought with me a history of our final destination, but I dare say that can be remedied in Marseilles."

He glanced at Norita.

"Then undoubtedly the book will be in French."

"I can read French," Norita replied. "In fact, I can also read Italian if we should find a book in Naples."

She looked up at him as she spoke, thinking perhaps she was being greedy in asking so much.

The Marquis, however, was thinking of the money he had spent on various women in the last few years, which came to a very large sum indeed.

Never before, though, had a woman asked him for a book!

"I will make a list of what you require," he said, moving towards his desk, "and I suggest you make a list for me of those you require for Alyce."

As he sat down he said:

"I suppose, if you are teaching her to be an artist, you will require paint-boxes and brushes?"

"There is one other thing, if I dare to suggest it, we need proper drawing-blocks."

"I think it would be easier if you made a list, however long it might be," the Marquis said.

"I will do that," Norita replied, "and thank you very much, My Lord. I am very, very grateful."

She made him a curtsy.

Then, before the Marquis could think of anything more to say, she had left his cabin.

When she had gone, he sat staring at the door through which she had just left.

He was thinking that the whole interview was not what he might have expected to have with a Governess.

"She is certainly different from anyone I have ever employed before!" he told himself, "but she certainly cares for Alyce, although it is obvious she despises me!"

He told himself, with a sarcastic twist of his lips, that that in itself was unusual.

Chapter Five

The Marquis's party came aboard at Marseilles.

Norita had one glance at them as they climbed up the gangway.

She realised that now things would be very different.

Because of what she had said to the Marquis, he had invited Alyce to have Luncheon with him every day.

Although she had tried to refuse, he had included her in the invitation.

She therefore found herself talking to the Marquis in the same way she had talked to her father.

She realised she had been wrong in thinking he was not intelligent or a reader.

In fact, she found every meal they had together a delight.

He did not ask her to dine with him, but the first evening after Alyce had been to Luncheon, he sent for her when Dinner was finished.

She had gone rather nervously into the Saloon, thinking perhaps something was wrong and he intended to find fault with her.

To her surprise he talked to her about Bahrain.

She found he knew a great deal about the pearl fishing and about pearls in general.

They discussed the great pearls of the world. The Oviedo Pearl found in Panama; the pearls of Mary Queen of Scots and of Queen Elizabeth.

These she loved so much that when she was about to die, she put on her great pearl necklaces and ear-rings to meet the Angel of Death.

The Marquis told Norita how the voluptuous Roman Emperor, Caligula, had decorated his favourite horse, Incitatus, with a pearl necklace.

Norita laughed and said:

"If I were a man, I would much rather give a pearl necklace to my horse than to some woman who would only enjoy it because of its value."

The Marquis raised his eyebrows.

"Why do you say that?"

"Because I have always been told that women prefer diamonds."

"And you, I suppose, prefer pearls."

"If I were fortunate enough to own one," Norita said, "I think because pearls mean something personal to me I would feel, as the Ancients believed, they were both inspiring and healing."

"They also, as you must be aware, have always expressed purity and perfection," the Marquis said, somewhat dryly.

He was thinking that certainly did not apply to Lady Bettine. Norita was following her own train of thought as she said:

"My Father told me once that the bronze statue of Aphrodite known as the Tyszkiewicz has been described as the most beautiful Venus ever known. She had a pearl suspended from the lobe of her ear."

The Marquis smiled.

"I think you would find it rather uncomfortable."

"But very beautiful," Norita replied.

They talked of other pearls which the Marquis had seen, and Norita listened to him attentively.

Then she said:

"You are so fortunate. You have been able to see things and go to places which I have found only in books."

"But now your patience has been rewarded," the Marquis replied, "and when we get to Bahrain you will see the pearls and, who knows, we might find the Perfect Pearl, which so many people have sought yet failed to find."

Norita's eyes twinkled.

"And are you prepared, My Lord, like the man in the Bible, to sell all you have and buy the Perfect Pearl?"

The Marquis thought for a moment. Then he said:

"That depends."

Norita waited, but he did not say any more.

* * *

Now the Marquis was waiting for Lady Bettine.

As she stepped on deck, Norita was sure she would be the recipient of the Perfect Pearl, should the Marquis find it.

She had never imagined that anyone could look so alluring.

Lady Bettine's beauty was enhanced by the sable cape she wore and a sable hat which framed her golden hair.

Norita did not miss the effusive way in which the Marquis's guests greeted him.

She thought Lady Malton was almost as beautiful as Lady Bettine.

Her chinchilla coat showed up her brilliant red hair and her green eyes to perfection.

There were other people in the party, but Norita suddenly realised she was watching them in a way her mother would not have approved.

Taking Alyce by the hand, they quickly went below to their own quarters.

Alyce was quite content to do so because she wanted to look at the books the Marquis had bought her earlier.

He had searched Marseilles for them and for two large paint-boxes.

He had bought an abundance of everything Norita had put on her list.

She knew he intended there would be plenty for them to do without interfering with his party.

She thought a little wistfully that they would be able to listen to him talking so intelligently while she might never have the chance again to pit her brain against his.

Then she told herself she was being greedy.

Who else would be so lucky as to be taken on this wonderful cruise and, as the Marquis had promised, to see the divers working in Bahrain?

They would be able to watch them searching for the pearls that had such an intriguing and exciting history.

The books which the Marquis had bought certainly increased her own knowledge about places they were passing.

They also contained pictures which delighted Alyce.

Even in the few days since she had been eating the Chef's brilliantly executed dishes, Alyce seemed more alert and happier.

Norita had offered him a challenge.

The Chef excelled himself in providing special dishes for the child that were different from anybody else's.

Some of them were so cleverly done that even the Marquis was intrigued.

The liver which Norita had asked for for Alyce was disguised in many ways.

Usually the food was already arranged on her plate, cut into the shape of a man, a horse or a basket and decorated with tomatoes cut into the shape of roses, shrimps in little boats or mushrooms.

On one dish they formed the ears of a rabbit.

Because Alyce was so delighted, she ate quite a lot of everything she was given.

Norita was sure the Chef was right when he said she would soon become a happy, laughing child.

Certainly every day she became more and more energetic, and Norita taught her to play Deck Tennis.

They took their exercise early in the morning before the Marquis's party was awake.

Then again, in the early afternoon, while they were still eating and drinking in the Saloon.

As Norita had predicted, they now saw very little of the Marquis.

She did not realise, and would not have understood if she had, that he had no wish for Bettine, Hermione, or indeed any other member of his party to see her.

He was well aware that first of all they would be astonished at her looks.

Then they would be suspicious as to why he had engaged such a young and lovely Governess.

He anticipated only too well the sort of jokes that would be made about Norita, and he had therefore hoped her presence on board would remain unnoticed.

It was Lady Langley who first discovered her.

Elizabeth Langley had always been worried about Alyce, and the Marquis's mother had talked to her about the child on several occasions.

"I suppose 'only children' always suffer from a lack of companionship," the Marchioness had said, "but Miss Marsh tells me it is difficult to find children of the same age at Hawk House where Alyce spends most of her time."

Lady Langley had therefore been surprised when she learned that Alyce was on board the *Sea Hawk*.

As they passed down the Mediterranean, she had made her way to Alyce's cabin.

She had been surprised when she reached the door to hear Alyce laughing and talking animatedly, which was something she could not remember her doing in the past.

Then, when she met Norita, she understood.

Later that evening, when she was alone with the Marquis, she said to him:

"There is such an improvement in Alyce that I can hardly believe it!"

"What do you mean?" the Marquis asked.

"I went to see her this morning," Lady Langley said. "I think her new Governess, whom I found extremely intelligent, has done marvels with the child. Need I say more?"

"That is what I thought myself," the Marquis replied.

Lady Langley paused for a moment. Then she said:

"I think you are wise to have put them at the other end of the yacht. I do not think Bettine is very fond of children."

There was no need to say more; the Marquis knew without words that she would not refer to Norita in front of the rest of the party.

As the yacht proceeded towards Egypt, he was regretting that he had brought two women who were interested in him on the same journey.

He would have been obtuse, which he was not, if he had not been aware that Bettine and Hermione's voices sharpened when they spoke to each other.

He also realised that Hermione was doing everything in her power to attract him.

He admired her and thought her very amusing.

At the same time, he had no wish to have two women fighting over him in a confined space.

By the time they reached Alexandria, he had decided that he was not enjoying the voyage as much as he had expected.

He found himself, quite unexpectedly, criticising Bettine's artificial mannerisms.

Also, when he was not paying her compliments or making love to her, she had little to say that was of any particular interest.

It was something that had not worried him before.

He had been beguiled by her beauty that was so outstanding, so he thought it unnecessary for her to have any other talents.

Now at mealtimes when he had Bettine on one side of him and Hermione on the other, he found himself thinking of the discussions he had enjoyed with Norita.

She always contributed something unusual to everything they talked about.

Or else she would ask him questions which required him to use his brains to find the right answer.

He looked at the elaborate and very glamorous creations which Bettine and Hermione wore every evening.

Yet he found himself wondering how he would dress Norita so as to portray her very unusual beauty to the best advantage.

He was aware that she wore the same worn and threadbare gown he had seen before, or else one that was equally shabby.

It was impossible to prevent himself from occasionally comparing her natural freshness and the untouched translucence of her skin with Bettine.

The latter used rouges, powder, mascara and dozens of little tricks to attract his attention.

He knew every one of them all too well.

The way she glanced at him provocatively from under her eyelashes, the inviting manner in which she moved her lips.

She invariably looked up at the sky so that she showed off the long line of her neck.

He was quite certain that Norita never gave a thought to her appearance.

Nor when he joined them unexpectedly, did she worry if her hair was untidy, having been blown about by the wind.

Her cheeks would be flushed without rouge because she had been playing with Alyce.

Her eyes were shining, not for him, but because she found everything they were doing so exciting.

"I have something to ask you, Papa," Alyce said as the

Marquis joined them on deck very early in the morning before the *Sea Hawk* docked at Alexandria.

"What is it?" the Marquis enquired.

"Miss Combe thinks I should give Chef a present to thank him for all those pretty dishes he has made for me."

"A good idea!" the Marquis said. "I will tell Johnson to let some of the traders, and there are dozens of them, bring their wares aboard so that you can choose what you would like to give him."

Alyce clapped her hands together.

"That is a lovely idea! And perhaps, Papa, I could buy a present for you!"

The Marquis looked surprised before he replied:

"Thank you, Alyce! It is something I would like very much!"

The child ran away from them along the deck and the Marquis turned to Norita to say:

"Is this a new sort of lesson?"

"I have found that Alyce has always accepted presents," Norita said quietly, "but she has never *given* any."

The Marquis thought for a moment. Then he said:

"To be honest, it never entered my mind. But of course, you are rightly pointing out that it is 'more blessed to give than to receive'!"

Norita did not answer.

The Marquis knew she was thinking that because he was so rich, it was something which was always expected of him.

He was surprised that he could read her thoughts.

He knew without being told that it had never crossed her mind that she herself might receive a gift either from Alyce, or himself.

It was something he quite unaccountably felt he wanted to rectify.

When the traders came aboard he sent for Alyce.

She came alone and he thought it sensible of Norita not

to come with her.

Bettine and Hermione vied with each other to find the finest, more luxurious gifts for the Marquis to buy them.

He, however, deliberately concentrated on Alyce and found a very attractive piece of Oriental carving which they thought the Chef would enjoy, as it depicted various fruits and fish.

"He will like that, I know he will!" Alyce said. "May I take it to him now?"

"There is somebody else for whom I think you should buy a gift," the Marquis said, "and that is Miss Combe."

"Yes, of course!" Alyce agreed. "What do you think she would like?"

One of the traders had shown Bettine and Hermione some very beautifully embroidered kaftans.

There was one the Marquis saw that was very much more expensive than the rest, and certainly very skilfully executed.

But it was too slim for either Bettine or Hermione. He was sure it would fit Norita, and he bought it and had it packed up for Alyce to take to her.

Then, so that Norita would not feel he had singled her out in any particular manner, he added an amusing corkscrew for Alyce to give to Johnson and another small gift for the Steward who waited on them.

Alyce then found a cigarette box inlaid with Mother of Pearl which she could give him.

Then she ran off with her other presents.

The Marquis could then get down to approving the enormous number of Egyptian goods that had been chosen by Bettine and Hermione and for which he was expected to pay.

They did not stay long at Alexandria, but moved into the Suez Canal.

It had grown very much hotter during the day, but was still cool at night.

Yet the Marquis thought with relief that he was not expected to wander about the deck gazing at the stars.

He therefore settled down to a game of Bridge with the three men he had chosen as his guests.

They were sitting at the Bridge Table when Sir Mortimer remarked:

"That is a very attractive young woman you have chosen as the Governess to your daughter!"

"As a matter of fact, I did not choose her," the Marquis corrected. "The Governess who had been with her for some time had to leave suddenly and I believe there was only a day or two for my Secretary to replace her before we left."

He spoke deliberately coldly, as he did not wish to discuss Norita.

He thought irritatedly that there was a faint smile on Sir Mortimer's lips, as if he did not believe him.

* * *

The following evening, as the Marquis was retiring to bed, his valet Hignet came to his cabin to say:

"I thinks, M'Lord, you should go to Her Ladyship's cabin. Miss Combe's frightened!"

"Frightened?" the Marquis asked sharply. "What has frightened her?"

"There's only two things, M'Lord, that women be frightened of," Hignet replied. "They be mice an' men, and there b'aint no mice on this ship!"

The Marquis, who had been taking off his evening-coat, shrugged it back on again and hurried from his cabin towards Alyce's Sitting-Room.

As he reached it he heard Sir Mortimer say:

"Now be a sensible girl! I am not going to hurt you! I only want to kiss you and tell you how lovely you are!"

"Go . . away . . and leave . . me alone!" Norita replied. "You have no . . right to come . . here."

"And who is going to stop me?" Sir Mortimer enquired.

The Marquis opened the door.

Sir Mortimer had his back to him. Norita was standing on the other side of the table wearing her dressing-gown, her fair hair falling over her shoulders.

She looked very young and very lovely as she faced Sir Mortimer defiantly.

In one hand she held a pair of scissors.

The Marquis noted that she was pointing them at her unwelcome visitor as if they were a weapon.

The Marquis took in everything in the passing of a second, then said in an ordinary tone:

"Ah, here you are, Mortimer! Hermione is asking for you. I said I would find you."

Sir Mortimer started when he heard the Marquis speak, then with an obvious effort he forced himself to say:

"If Hermione wants me I had better go to her. I wonder what is wrong?"

"I am sure she will tell you when you reach her," the Marquis remarked with a touch of sarcasm in his voice.

Then Sir Mortimer said:

"Good-night, Miss Combe, and I hope you will play Deck Tennis with me tomorrow."

With that he walked from the cabin with a jaunty air which did not deceive the Marquis.

Norita stood still until she heard his footsteps die away. Then she said in a hesitant little voice:

"H .. he .. frightened .. me!"

The Marquis shut the cabin door.

"I am sorry."

Norita did not seem to hear him.

She put the scissors down on the table and sat down in a chair.

The Marquis saw the pile of muslin on it and guessed she had been making herself a gown.

There was a chair opposite Norita and he sat down in it.

He was aware as he did so that she was looking very pale, and as she clasped her hands together he saw that she was trembling.

"Now do not be upset about this. . ." he began.

"I . . I want . . to go h . . home," Norita said, "but . . I suppose it would be difficult . . and I may not . . have enough money."

She was talking as if she was thinking it out for herself, and the Marquis replied:

"There is no reason to be upset."

"But . . there is!" Norita interrupted. "I . . I did not . . realise there were . . men in the world who would . . talk to me like that . . when they have . . never even . . met me!"

"What did Sir Mortimer say to you?" the Marquis asked sharply.

"H . . he said he thought I was . . very pretty . . and he wanted to . . kiss me . . look after me . . and . . give me . . presents."

The words came haltingly from her lips. Then she said:

"He . . he has never even . . spoken to me before!"

The Marquis realised she found what had happened completely incomprehensible.

After a moment he said very quietly:

"Now listen, you have to think this out for yourself. Because you are very pretty — no — lovely is the right word — you will find men wherever you go who will want to tell you so."

"Men I . . do not . . know?" Norita asked.

"All men, whoever they are, are attracted to beauty," the Marquis said. "You have read a lot, and you must have found that happens in books, if nothing else!"

"I suppose it . . would in . . novels," she replied, "but I have not read many. I read only what Papa and I were interested in — History and the people of other lands. In fact . . I find novels rather . . boring."

"You are upset simply because you are so young," the

Marquis answered. "When you grow older, you will find, Norita, that men want to talk to you about love."

Norita looked at him. Then she said:

"That is not love . . that is not . . real love. I think it is something . . insulting and also . . very frightening!"

"Why?" the Marquis could not help asking.

"Because . . although I may be wrong . . if one loves a person . . one would love them for themselves . . not for how they . . l . . look."

The Marquis smiled.

"Men, as you well know, have searched for Aphrodite all down the ages."

"But they are seeking 'real love'," Norita argued, "which makes a man do glorious deeds for the woman he loves, and she will do anything, even die . . if necessary . . to save him from being hurt."

Her voice was very moving.

It flashed through the Marquis's mind that he had never known a love that was like that.

He knew what Norita was saying was to her very real.

"That is the love that we all hope we shall find," he said quietly. "It is rather like the perfect pearl, and one may spend a lifetime being disappointed."

"Do you mean . . one never finds . . it?" Norita asked.

"Love is like the stars overhead. We cannot touch them, but we know they are there, and as they are in themselves perfection, so we must always strive towards them."

The Marquis was surprised at himself.

Yet he supposed such ideals had always been in his heart, although he had never before expressed them.

There was silence until Norita asked in a lost little voice:

"What shall I . . do about that . . man?"

"Nothing!" the Marquis said firmly. "He will not trouble you again. I will see to that!"

"You are . . quite sure?"

"Quite sure! At the same time, I think you should lock

your door after Alyce has gone to bed."

"I .. I will do that .. but I do want to .. look at the .. stars!"

"Is that what you do every night?"

"They are .. so beautiful, and now you tell me they are what we must aim for, I understand why it lifts my heart just to look at them."

The Marquis smiled.

"Then you must certainly look at the stars, and I promise you I will keep Sir Mortimer busy at the card-table."

Norita smiled and it transformed her frightened little face as if the sun had suddenly come out.

Then she said:

"I did not want to .. make a scene .. but I suppose .. really .. I should not have .. come on this .. journey."

The Marquis was aware that wherever she went, looking as she did, there would always be men like Mortimer Garson who would pursue her and try to spoil her.

He suddenly felt a surge of anger that any man should touch or despoil anything so young, so innocent and so completely pure.

He rose to his feet.

"Leave everything to me," he said. "I promise you will not be disturbed again and thank you for all you have done for Alyce. She is a different child!"

Norita rose too.

The Marquis thought that with her hair falling over her shoulders how young she looked.

At the same time, indescribably lovely.

"I think," Norita said hesitatingly, "I .. I should thank .. Your Lordship for the .. present Alyce .. bought me."

"It fitted you?"

Norita blushed.

"I feel .. very Egyptian in it .. but .. perhaps Mama would be .. shocked at my accepting such a .. present. . ."

She looked at him questioningly, and as the Marquis did not answer she went on:

"I am . . sure I . . ought to say . . no, but Alyce would be so . . hurt."

"I think it would be very unkind," the Marquis agreed, "if you refused one of the first presents she has ever given."

"Then . . you think it is . . right for me to . . keep it?"

"Absolutely right," the Marquis said firmly. "And it would be very hurtful of you to refuse."

"Then . . thank you . . thank you very much!"

The Marquis knew that she was in fact thrilled at having anything so lovely to wear and her eyes expressed exactly what she was feeling.

She had deferred to him for his approval as if to her he was a Father-figure.

She looked so lovely as she did so that he wanted to take her in his arms and tell her he would protect her so that no one would frighten her again.

Then he was both surprised and shocked at his own reaction.

To relieve the tension he looked down at the pile of muslin embroidered with little blue flowers on the table and said:

"I imagine you are making yourself a gown."

"I ought to . . thank Your Lordship for that . . too."

"Thank me?" the Marquis enquired.

"Your Housekeeper, Mrs. Winter, gave it to me when we were at Hawk House, because there was no time for me to go shopping and my dresses really are a disgrace!"

Having explained herself, Norita glanced at the Marquis pleadingly as she went on:

"You do not think it . . wrong of me to have accepted . . the muslin from Mrs. Winter?"

"No, of course not!" the Marquis said, "and I shall look forward to seeing you in the gown you have made yourself."

He saw Norita's eyes light up for a moment, then she looked away and said:

"You do not think . . if I wear anything . . smart like the kaftan . . or a new gown that. . . ?"

"Certainly not!" the Marquis said firmly. "I have told you Sir Mortimer will not come near you, and I can assure you, Norita, that he will obey me!"

He did not realise he had used her Christian name, but the relief on Norita's face was very touching.

"Now go to bed," the Marquis said, "you have worked enough for tonight, and everything will seem better in the morning. It will not be long now before we reach Bahrain."

Then, because Norita's eyes seemed to shine like stars, he knew that was what she was looking forward to.

Opening the door, he said again:

"Go to bed, and do not worry about anything!"

"Thank . . you! Thank you . . very much!"

The Marquis walked back to his own cabin and undressed without speaking to Hignet.

It was only when he was ready to get into bed that he said:

"You were right to tell me that Miss Combe was upset, Hignet, and I hope you will keep an eye on her. She is far too young for the position she is in."

"That's wot I thinks meself, M'Lord," Hignet replied, "an' a nicer, more pleasant young Lady would be 'ard to find anywhere in th' world!"

The Marquis was surprised.

Hignet had been with him for a long time, and he had never known him make a mistake about anybody's status in the domestic hierarchy.

He knew that Hignet referred to Miss Marsh as 'a nice woman', and when he used the word 'Lady' he confirmed what he had already thought himself.

That Norita was not an ordinary Governess, but a Lady.

He had known it, he thought, when they talked together at Luncheon and again in the evenings after Dinner.

She had never made a mistake, ever since she had been with him.

She had never done anything which would not have been perfectly right in the most distinguished Drawing-Rooms of Mayfair.

"If she is a Lady," he told himself as he got into bed, "then obviously she has only become a Governess because she needs the money!"

It seemed extraordinary that she should not have relatives or friends who could look after her as might be expected in an ordinary family.

'She is certainly very intelligent,' he thought as he lay in the darkness, 'and very beautiful!'

He had wondered before how long her hair was when she had worn it in a coil at the back of her head.

Now he knew it fell over her shoulders and down to her breasts.

"Dammit!" he told himself, "I should not be thinking of her like this! After all, I employ her as my daughter's Governess!"

He turned over restlessly and, as he did so, the door opened.

He knew who it was before he heard a soft, deliberately sweet voice say:

"Darling Selwyn, I could not sleep, and you did not come to say goodnight to me!"

It was Bettine, and the Marquis held out his hand invitingly.

He wanted to forget what he had been thinking.

He wanted to concentrate, as he was expected to do, on the Beauty he had brought on this voyage so that he could give her some pearls.

Chapter Six

BY THE time the *Sea Hawk* had steamed through the Red Sea into the Gulf of Aden, then on to the Indian Ocean and into the Gulf of Oman, the Marquis was bored.

He was bored with Bettine's constant demands for his attention and expressions of love.

He was bored by the way that Hermione pursued him so obviously that Perry and George were laughing about it.

He was bored too with the conversation at mealtimes, which was dominated by the Beauties on his right and left being perpetually spiteful to one another.

He felt the only thing that was good about the voyage was Alyce.

From being a dull, listless, unprepossessing child, she had become animated, obstreperous and obviously very happy.

He knew it was all due to Norita, but he did not wish to think of her if he could help it.

It was impossible, however, not to do so.

Early in the morning he exercised himself before his party was awake, and found Norita and Alyce were doing the same thing.

They were at the far end of the yacht so that any noise they made could not be heard in the State Cabins occupied by Bettine and Hermione.

But the Marquis could hear their laughter and the excitement in their young voices before he reached them.

When he did so, Alyce ran towards him eagerly and,

when he bent down to pick her up, she put her arms around his neck.

"It is so lovely to be here, Papa," she had said to him this morning, "and I saw a Mermaid in the sea!"

The Marquis suspected it was a dolphin but he replied:

"I am sure there are lots of Mermaids and perhaps they, like you, are looking for pearls."

"Shall I be able to dive to find them?" Alyce asked.

"You will find it much more comfortable to watch the real divers, who are very experienced at bringing up the oysters."

When they reached Bahrain, Norita and Alyce gasped at the enormous number of fishing-boats they could see everywhere.

In one of the books which the Marquis had bought, Norita had read a report made three years ago which said there were 1,500 boats in Bahrain.

There were also a large number along the Pirate Coast which was situated between Bahrain and the Gulf of Oman.

Alyce was immediately interested in pirates.

Norita learned from Johnson that the Wahabis of the Pirate Coast had come under the persuasive influence of British gunboats and magazine-rifles.

They had now substituted pearling for their two-centuries-long life of fanatical piracy.

They had not only been notorious for this, but also because they murdered their captives, explaining:

"It is written in the Koran that it is not lawful to plunder the living, but we are not prohibited from stripping the dead."

Norita did not tell Alyce about this, but tried to make her concentrate on the fishing-boats and the divers, who were mostly Arabs.

Bahrain was a mixture of ancient and modern.

Naked children romped in the shallow water.

There were a few crude houses surmounted by square wind-turrets. The rest were the square, white Arab dwellings.

Behind them, the Marquis knew, there were the *Suqs*.

These were covered passage-ways where merchants sat in the gloom, cross-legged in narrow alcoves, haggling over pearls.

Many races wandered in the *Suqs* — pallid Arab townsmen, quick-eyed armed *Bedou*.

There were also Negro slaves, Daluchis, Persian and Indian buyers.

The *Sea Hawk* anchored on the coast, some distance from the town.

Early the first morning, Norita and Alyce were watching the fishing-boats moving into position for their divers.

The Marquis joined them.

"I have just learned," he said, "that in Bahrain there are nearly 35,000 fishermen, but we will not see so many at work at the moment."

"Why not?" Norita enquired.

"Because it is too early in the year," the Marquis explained. "Most divers prefer to work between June and September, when the water is warmer."

Norita realised that while the sun was hot in the day, it could be much cooler at night.

Yet still very much warmer than it would have been in Europe.

"Surely we shall see some diving?" she asked quickly.

She thought it would be too disappointing to have come all this way and see nothing but boats.

The Marquis looked a little ahead of them and said:

"Suppose we go and see now, before the rest of the party is awake?"

He put out his hand to Alyce, who was dancing with delight as he took them a little way along the water-front.

The fishermen were getting their boats ready.

The divers were carrying their stones which weighed from thirty to fifty pounds, depending on the depth of the water.

They were all oval-shaped and perforated at one end to admit a rope.

This was fixed to the diver's waist.

The Marquis talked to one of the ferrymen who was directing the diving.

He explained in broken English that the diver, when sinking beneath the surface of the water, crouched down in a stooping position.

He collected as many oysters as possible during the fifty seconds in which he was able to remain under water.

When Alyce saw a man come to the surface puffing and blowing, she clapped her hands with delight.

They then looked at the contents of the large basket.

The diver's assistant was separating dead shells and refuse from the live oysters.

"You must realise," the Marquis said to his daughter, "that the diver has to work very quickly, while he holds his breath. He picks up everything within reach, including, as you can see, some rubbish."

"There are lots of good oysters too, Papa!" Alyce cried.

With a smile, Norita suggested that she count them.

They were so fascinated by the boats, the divers and the oysters they kept bringing to the surface that the Marquis forgot the time.

They were joined long before he had expected it by Perry, Sir Mortimer and, to his consternation, Bettine.

He was aware that Norita stiffened as Sir Mortimer approached them and moved with Alyce away from the group.

Some new divers had just begun to work only a short distance from the shore.

It was easy for them to watch and see exactly what happened.

Norita deliberately did not look back, hoping that Sir Mortimer would not notice her.

He had, in fact, been sulking ever since the Marquis had warned him to leave her alone.

"Really, Selwyn!" he had said, "you are being very high-handed, unless of course you are interested in such a young and pretty person yourself!"

The Marquis had frowned and said in his most icy voice, which frightened most people:

"I do not interfere with my own servants or anybody else's, and that also applies to my guests!"

Sir Mortimer had walked away without replying.

But he had been extremely surly that evening, although the Marquis ignored his behaviour.

He was, however, relieved that Sir Mortimer had obviously not told Bettine or Hermione there was another Beauty on board.

He had hoped, because Elizabeth Langley was so tactful, that no one else would have any idea what Alyce's Governess looked like.

Then, unexpectedly, because she never rose before noon, Bettine was beside him.

"Why did you not tell me you were coming so early to watch the divers?" she asked plaintively.

She slipped her arm through the Marquis's and looked up at him.

"I intended to bring you later," he replied, "after asking the British Resident which was the best place on the coast for the largest pearls."

He forced himself to smile before he added:

"That is what you want, is it not, Bettine? Really large pearls to take home with you."

"I want a whole necklace of them!" Bettine replied, "and if you give anyone larger pearls than you give me, I shall be very angry!"

She glanced back at the *Sea Hawk* as she spoke, but

there was no sign of Hermione.

Then, moving a little closer to the Marquis, she said:

"Darling Selwyn, I want to look like the Maharajah of Patiala who, I believe, has the largest collection of pearls in the world!"

The Marquis laughed.

"In which case I think you will have to make love to the Maharajah, because his pearls have taken centuries to collect."

Bettine was frowning, as if he were depriving her of something she desired.

The Marquis, with a hasty glance at Norita who was some distance away, thought it wise to move back towards the yacht.

"What we are going to do," he said, "is wait to see the British Resident, then you and I, Bettine, will go out in a boat from which they are diving."

He paused to add impressively:

"You can then make certain you have first choice of the largest pearls that are brought aboard."

Bettine accepted this as being a good idea.

They strolled back to the yacht, followed by Sir Mortimer and Perry.

Norita was aware that they had left and heaved a sigh of relief.

She knew instinctively that the Marquis had no wish for his lady guests to see her.

She thought it was because she was so young that they might criticise his choice of a Governess.

She was too unselfconscious to suspect that any man, least of all the Marquis, would compare her with Lady Bettine, who was a famous Beauty.

Or Lady Hermione, whose red hair and green eyes must, she thought, command attention wherever she went.

Because Alyce was feeling so well and so energetic, they had walked almost to the tip of the Island.

Here there were only a few fishing-boats.

The sides of the cliff rose above deeper water than where they had watched the diving.

Then, as Norita stared at the sea which in the morning sun was the deep blue of the Madonna's robe, there was a shout.

Looking down, she saw just beneath them there were some men holding up a collection of oysters.

"Verry beeg pearls, Lady!" one man shouted.

Alyce gave a little cry of excitement.

"Some big pearls for Papa, Miss Combe!" she said. "Let us go and see if they are as big as Cleopatra's ear-ring."

Norita saw there was a twisting path leading down to the beach.

Because Alyce was so excited they went carefully down the side of the cliff.

It was not very high, and they reached the sandy beach below, on which there was a large fishing-boat, quite easily. Its bow was beached on the sand.

The man who had shouted to them showed them the oysters, and there were six other men in the boat watching them.

"You come verry beeg yacht?" he asked pointing to where, what seemed a long distance away, there was the *Sea Hawk*.

"I want to see your big pearls," Alyce said, "very, very big ones!"

"We have verry beeg ones in the boat," the Arab said. "Leetle Lady come aboard, we show."

"No, I think we must go back now," Norita replied.

She was too late.

Alyce had run to the half-beached *dhow*.

An Arab who was standing there was lifting her in his arms to put her down inside.

Another Arab sitting cross-legged had some pearls in his hand and Alyce went to look at them.

111

"Come back, Alyce!" Norita called. "I think we should return or your father will wonder where we are!"

"Come and look at these pearls, Miss Combe! There are lots of them, but they are not very big."

It was obvious Alyce was entranced by what she was shown.

An Arab put out his hand to help Norita aboard, and after a moment's hesitation she grasped it.

She moved carefully over the wet deck to where Alyce was standing by the Arab who was showing her the pearls.

There were, as she had said, quite a number of them. Several were large and had a beautiful lustre to them.

"Shall we take them back to Papa?" Alyce asked eagerly.

"I think. . ." Norita began.

As she spoke, the ship moved beneath her and she realised the Arabs were pushing it off the sand and out into the sea.

She turned to say quickly:

"The little girl and I must return immediately to the yacht!"

The Arab who spoke English replied:

"That ees eempossible, Lady! You our prisoners!"

As he spoke, the sails billowed out in the wind.

Norita started to protest but the Arab refused to listen.

Then she realised with horror that they were being carried, not only out to sea, but to the South.

The boat was heading towards the Pirate Coast which they had passed the previous day.

* * *

The Marquis escorted Bettine back to the yacht.

He was aware she had come to find him before breakfast and took her into the Saloon.

Because he was relieved she had not noticed Norita,

being so intent on the pearls he was to buy her, he made himself charming.

He hoped she would find him irresistible and forget everything else.

He paid her compliments while Sir Mortimer and Perry were still some way behind them.

When they came to join them it was to say that they were both hungry.

It was not until they had been aboard the yacht for nearly an hour that the Marquis began to wonder if his daughter was back.

He suddenly had the strangest feeling that she — or was it Norita? — was calling for him.

Because it seemed so insistent he said to Johnson, who was waiting on them at breakfast:

"Find out if Her Ladyship has returned."

"Very good, M'Lord."

Johnson went from the cabin and was away so long that the Marquis wondered what was keeping him.

When he came back he said:

"The Captain wants to speak to Your Lordship!"

There was something in the way Johnson spoke which told the Marquis it was urgent.

He rose quickly and went out on deck where the Captain was waiting for him.

"What is it?" he asked.

"I don't wish to alarm you, M'Lord," the Captain said, "but one of our seamen has just reported seeing Her Ladyship and Miss Combe aboard a vessel which was taking them South."

"What sort of vessel?" the Marquis asked sharply.

"It was a large fishing-boat, M'Lord, and the man thinks it came from the Pirate Coast!"

The Marquis saw by the expression on the Captain's face exactly what he was thinking.

He said sharply:

"Get me a vehicle of some sort! I must contact the British Resident immediately!"

The Captain sent a seaman running into the Town and, while the Marquis waited on deck, Perry came to join him.

"What has happened?" he asked.

"It seems unlikely," the Marquis said, "but the Captain suspects that Alyce and Miss Combe have been carried off in a fishing-boat to the Pirate Coast."

Perry stared at him.

"I do not believe it!"

"There may be quite a reasonable explanation," the Marquis said, "but they were seen travelling in that direction, and the pirates will be well aware they can demand a large ransom for my daughter!"

"Good God!" Perry exclaimed. "How could we imagine anything like that could happen here?"

"It is something I should have anticipated," the Marquis said.

He did not speak angrily, but in a cold, icy voice. It made Perry know that he was furious and at the same time undoubtedly apprehensive.

It was only a short time before the seaman returned with a very old, dilapidated-looking open carriage.

It had obviously been in use for many years, but it had four wheels and the horse drawing it was young and capable of running quickly.

The Marquis and Perry reached the British Residency in what was record time, although it seemed like the passing of a century.

They were received immediately by Colonel Ross who held out his hand saying:

"Welcome, My Lord! I was just about to call on you!"

"My daughter and her Governess have been kidnapped!" the Marquis said abruptly. "One of the seamen aboard my yacht reported seeing them on a ship sailing towards the Pirate Coast!"

Colonel Ross, who was a distinguished man, looked at him in astonishment.

"I can hardly believe it!"

"It is true," the Marquis said, "and I want to know what can be done about it!"

"The first thing is to ascertain if the intention is to hold them prisoner, and it would be wisest if we waited until they demanded a ransom!"

"I have no intention of waiting!" the Marquis said. "If you cannot act immediately, then I shall have to do so with my own crew!"

"I understand your anxiety, My Lord," the Colonel said, "and I will send for the Officer in Command of the Troop and ask his advice."

"Thank you," the Marquis said. "I feel it is imperative that there should be no delay."

The way he spoke made Perry aware that he was determined to galvanise Colonel Ross and everybody else in Bahrain into taking action.

* * *

As they sailed away, moving because the wind was behind them far quicker than Norita expected, she thought despairingly that it was her fault.

She had taken Alyce away from the Marquis when Sir Mortimer had joined him.

She had not seen him since the night he had come to the cabin and frightened her.

She had thought it would have been very embarrassing if he had singled her out in front of Lady Bettine and Captain Napier.

Ever since that night, she had locked her door as the Marquis had instructed her to do.

She had also been aware that Hignet always seemed to be around when Alyce had been put to bed.

Because the valet was such a kind man she found it impossible not to let him talk to her in a way which made him sound like a consoling Nanny.

"Now don't you worrit yourself, Miss," he said not once but half-a-dozen times. "If His Lordship tells the gent'men they're not to come 'ere, they won't!"

"How can you be sure of that?" Norita asked.

"The Master always gets his own way," Hignet replied, "and anyone as offends 'im ain't asked again to Hawk House in London, nor to His Lordship's Palace in the country."

"Palace?" Norita questioned.

"That's wot you'll think it is when you see it! Bigger than Blenheim, an' much more comfortable — an' I speaks from experience!"

Norita laughed.

It was then impossible to go on being frightened if both the Marquis and Hignet were watching over her.

Now, she thought, Alyce was in danger, and the Marquis would be very angry when he knew they had been abducted.

They were, she thought, about an hour's journey from the port.

Then she was suddenly desperately afraid that they might be killed, as the Wahabis had killed their captives in the past.

She was, however, quite bright enough to know that was because the pirates had taken prisoner those who either had a lot of money, or a great number of pearls on them.

She and Alyce had nothing of value except themselves.

It was therefore stupid to be afraid, even though she could not help it.

Because she was also afraid of being hit on the head by a sail when the ship changed direction, she sat down on the deck.

Alyce joined her.

"What is happening, Miss Combe?" she asked. "Why are these men taking us away in their ship?"

"I think they are pirates, dearest," Norita replied, "but I am sure your Father will soon rescue us."

"Pirates?" Alyce exclaimed. "But they have no red handkerchiefs on their heads!"

"All the same, I think that is what they are," Norita said, "and you must be very brave and behave with dignity because you are English."

"If they are .. taking me away from Papa .. I am frightened!" Alyce protested.

"So am I," Norita agreed, "but your Father would want us to be very brave, and not show them that we are afraid."

Alyce considered this for some time, then she said:

"Papa is very brave! He was given a Medal when he was in the Army!"

Norita thought it was what she might have expected.

Everything she had thought about the Marquis before she knew him was wrong.

She knew now that he was clever, authoritative and so ingenious that somehow he would get them back without either of them being hurt.

Nevertheless, she put her arm around Alyce and held her close.

They went quite a long way down the Pirate Coast before they entered a small bay.

Norita could see no sign of any houses or any human habitation on the land above them.

She thought then with a sinking heart that it might be impossible for the Marquis to find out where they were.

Finally the boat was grounded and the Arab who spoke English said:

"Ladees come 'shore!"

"Where are we going?" Norita asked. "I demand an explanation as to why you have brought us here!"

117

"Tell you everytheeng when you 'shore," the Arab answered.

Because she was frightened her defiance would cause them to be taken off the ship physically, Norita allowed herself to be helped down onto the sand.

The Arab then lifted Alyce in his arms and set her down beside her.

Then they were led a short distance to where, hidden from the sea by a projecting rock, there was a rough indent in the cliffs.

In the centre of it there was a flat surface of sand.

There was nothing else to see and Norita stood waiting, knowing she was growing more and more afraid.

Then the Arabs behind them came up with what she realised was a small black tent, the same as those used by the *Bedou*.

They erected it swiftly and competently on the flat ground between the rocks.

Norita saw it was very small and would be impossible for anyone to stand upright inside.

When it was completed the Arab said:

"Ladees go eenside — cannot escape. Someone watch all the time you heere!"

"If we are to stay here any length of time," Norita said, "I hope you intend to give us some food. This little girl will be hungry!"

The Arab considered this for a moment. Then he said:

"I breeng food if you pay me."

Norita looked at him helplessly.

"With what?" she answered. "I have no money."

The Arab made no reply and she said:

"If you intend to ask a ransom of us you can add the money to the sum you are demanding."

The Arab showed a flash of his white teeth.

"Good idee!" he said. "Gentleman pay big money for little girl an' preety ladee — and food."

118

"I hope you will get what you ask," Norita said coldly. "In the meantime, we want food, and surely you have some fruit which will quench our thirst."

The Arab looked at her. Then he said as if he wished to show his authority:

"Ladees go een tent!"

Because there was nothing else they could do, Norita knelt down and crawled inside the tent and Alyce followed her.

There was a rug on the ground which she thought the Muslims used when they prayed.

Otherwise there was nothing but darkness.

The Arab then fastened the entrance to the tent and Alyce asked in a frightened voice:

"How long shall we be here, Miss Combe? I do not like it, and I want to go back to Papa!"

Norita held Alyce close against her.

Then, because there seemed to be nothing else she could do, she started to pray that they would soon be saved and the Marquis would know where to find them.

"Help us .. help us!" she prayed to God and to her father and mother.

Then, because it seemed the natural thing to do, she tried to tell the Marquis how much they wanted him.

Her father had often described to her the way the Indians communicated to each other over great distances by the power of thought.

Now Norita felt as if she was sending up a cry which the Marquis could not fail to hear.

"Save us! Save us!" she was crying in her mind and in her heart.

Then she talked to Alyce, but it seemed a long time before there was a sound outside the tent and the flap was unfastened.

Both Norita and Alyce were very hot as there was no air, and they were also very thirsty.

"I breeng food," the Arab said.

"Thank you," Norita replied, "and while we are eating, could you leave the tent open? If we die of suffocation no one will pay you for us."

The Arab grinned, but he left the flap open.

The food was what she might have expected — meatballs of lamb or goat and rice moistened with butter.

It did not look or taste very appetising, and was something which Alyce would certainly not have eaten a fortnight ago.

But now, with Norita's encouragement, she found it amusing to eat with her fingers the meatballs which had started by being hot and were now only tepid.

The fruit, two oranges and several small pomegranates, quenched their thirst.

While they were eating the Arab sat cross-legged outside the tent with a rifle on his knees.

But at least the tent was open and there was a slight breeze coming from the sea beyond the rocks.

When they had eaten, the Arab shut them in again and Alyce began to grow tearful.

"I do not like this place," she grumbled. "It is hot . . it is dark . . and I want to be back in the yacht with Papa!"

"What we have to do," Norita said, "is to think out a lovely story about this adventure. We will write it, and draw pictures of the boat which brought us here, and the bad Arabs who have taken us prisoner."

"Will that be a book?" Alyce enquired.

"It will be in the book you are going to give to your Grandmother, and I know she will be very excited to read what happened, and also how brave you were."

"Am I being brave?" Alyce asked.

"Very, very brave, and when your Papa comes he will be very proud of you."

"I wish Papa would hurry!" Alyce said.

Norita was wishing the same thing.

She wondered how long it would take the Arabs to sail their ship back to Bahrain and demand the ransom.

She was sure it would be an exorbitant sum.

The day seemed to drag on. The Arab did not bring them any more food until late in the evening, and Alyce was nearly asleep.

Norita had told her stories all the afternoon, but even they had begun to pall.

Then the Arab brought them the same food they had had before, except there was fish instead of meatballs.

"Eef you try escape in the dark we kill you — understand?"

"How can we escape?" Norita asked, "and anyway, we do not know where we are. If you were a kind man, because it is so hot and stuffy inside this tent, you would leave it open, and we will give you our word we will not run away."

The Arab considered this for a moment, then he asked: "You pay me?"

"Yes, I pay you," Norita said, "but it will have to be on the ransom!"

He laughed.

"I want money now!"

He shut the tent as he spoke and Norita knew there was nothing she could do but try to make Alyce comfortable.

She lay down on the ground and held the little girl in her arms so that she could sleep against her breast.

As she did so she wondered if one day she would hold her own child in the same way.

It flashed through her mind that it would be wonderful to have a son who was as handsome and clever as the Marquis.

Then she told herself it was something that would never happen.

So it would be best not to think about it, and yet it was impossible to keep him from encroaching on her mind.

During the day she had told Alyce story after story until her voice had grown quite hoarse.

Yet at the same time she was still sending her thoughts on wings towards the Marquis.

She begged him to save them, tried to tell him where they were.

Now she began to think despairingly that perhaps the Marquis would hand over the ransom money, however large the demand might be.

Then the pirates might revert to their old trick of killing their captives because the Koran had not said it was wrong to do so.

"Please . . God . . save us!" Norita said in a panic.

As she did so there was a sudden explosion that sounded like a shot, followed by another and yet another.

There was the sudden scream of a man in pain, followed by several more shots.

Norita laid Alyce on the ground and half-covered her with her body.

Then there was silence.

It flashed through her mind that perhaps the shots had not come from those who had come to save them, but from a rival pirate crew.

Then there was the sound of heavy footsteps and as she trembled she was aware that somebody was untying the tent-flat.

"Alyce! Norita!"

Only two words spoken in a voice she knew, and Norita gave a cry of joy.

It was the Marquis.

She pushed Alyce forward and the child crawled out of the tent.

"Papa! Papa! You have come!" she was crying. "It has been horried in here, and so hot! Please, Papa, take us home!"

"That is what I intend to do," the Marquis replied.

As he held Alyce in his arms he put out his free hand towards Norita, and taking it, she pulled herself to her feet.

"You are all right?" he asked.

"Everything .. is all right .. now that .. you have come," she answered.

To her surprise it was quite bright outside the tent.

There was a full moon and the stars, more brilliant than in any other part of the world, seemed to form a huge arc of light above them.

For a moment Norita could see only the Marquis.

Then, as their eyes met, his told her without words how worried he had been.

His fingers tightened on hers and without meaning to she moved a little closer to him.

"They have not hurt you?"

His voice was tense.

"No .. no .. we are .. all right," Norita said, "but very .. very glad that .. you are .. here!"

Now she looked round and saw that the Arab who had been sitting outside their tent was lying dead.

Two other Arabs had been shot and several more were being marched away by soldiers in British uniforms.

"Come along, I will take you back to the yacht," the Marquis said.

Alyce had her arms around his neck and Norita was still holding onto his hand.

There was a path through the rocks behind them and he led them up onto the flat ground above it.

There she saw in the distance a carriage drawn by two horses and also a Brake drawn by four, which she knew had brought the soldiers.

The Marquis took them over the flat, sandy ground to the carriage.

He lifted Alyce in first then, as Norita joined them, he sat between them.

There was an Officer giving orders to his men who were

123

bringing back the Arabs who were prisoners.

The Marquis did not speak to him as somebody shut the carriage door and they drove off.

Alyce, who was half-asleep, cuddled against her father.

"I am so . . glad you are here . . Papa! It was . . horrid in that . . black tent . . but Miss Combe told me lots and lots of . . stories."

"I thought that was what she would be doing," the Marquis said in a low voice.

He had released Norita's hand when they had reached the carriage.

Now he put his arm around her and somehow it seemed a natural thing for her to rest her head against him.

She did not remember that she and Alyce had left their bonnets in the tent.

She was, in fact, very near to tears from the fear she had been feeling.

The long hours in which they had been imprisoned made her feel that she wanted to cry on the Marquis's shoulder.

She would then tell him how glad she was that he had saved them.

Her eyes misted over, and although she wiped her tears away impatiently with the back of her hand, he was aware of what she was feeling.

"It is all right," he said gently, "and this will never happen again!"

"It . . was my . . fault," Norita said, "for taking . . Alyce so far . . away from you . . but. . ."

She wondered how she could explain that she did not wish to encounter Sir Mortimer, but there was no need for words.

"I understand," the Marquis interrupted, "and I should not have let you go, but how could I have imagined for one moment those devils were thinking of how to take you prisoner?"

"They were not cruel to us," Norita said, "but I kept remembering what the . . Wahabis used to do to their captives!"

"Did you think I did not remember it too?" the Marquis asked and there was a frantic note in his voice.

His arm tightened around her.

"I thought . . somehow you . . would find . . us," Norita said. "I prayed and . . tried to . . send you my . . thoughts like the . . Indians do."

"I knew that," the Marquis said. "I felt you calling me and, thank God, a man on duty at the Residency who reports to Colonel Ross the movement of every ship arriving and leaving the port saw you."

"Saw us?" Norita exclaimed.

"He watched your boat through his telescope and told me where the pirates had taken you."

"That must have . . made it . . easier," Norita said with a little sigh.

"Very much easier," the Marquis agreed, "but we knew it would be a mistake to strike before it was dark otherwise the Arabs would be aware of our approach from the land."

"It was . . wonderful of . . you to . . save us as . . you did!" Norita said.

"I would have blown up the whole damned place if I had been unable to do so!" the Marquis said.

There was a note of fury in his voice which told Norita that he meant what he had said.

She told herself that she had been mistaken in thinking he did not love his child.

Of course he loved Alyce, and it must have been an agony for him waiting for the hours to pass, just as it had been agony for her, waiting for his arrival.

"I am so . . glad you did . . not have to pay a . . large ransom," she murmured.

"I would have paid a million pounds and more, if it had been necessary," the Marquis replied. "Surely you know that where you two are concerned, money is unimportant?"

Norita looked up at him with a little smile and he added:

"Having found the Perfect Pearl, I was prepared to sell everything I owned so that I could possess it!"

Chapter Seven

It took them a long time to get back to the *Sea Hawk* and as they did so Perry came hurrying down the gangway to say:

"Thank God, you have found them! You were so long that I began to worry that something had gone wrong."

"Everything is all right," the Marquis said. "They are unhurt."

He handed the sleeping Alyce into Perry's arms, then, as Norita was ready to follow him, the Marquis said:

"I think Alyce should be put straight to bed, and there is no reason for you to talk to anybody."

"I do not . . wish . . to," Norita replied in a low voice.

She got out of the carriage and hurried up the gangway and past the Saloon.

She guessed the rest of the party were waiting there to hear what had happened.

Perry carried Alyce below and into her own cabin.

He put the child gently down on the bed and as Norita joined them he said:

"It must have been a terrible experience. They did not threaten you?"

"No, we were all right," Norita replied. "Only frightened!"

"I can understand that," he said, "and I think you are very brave!"

He left, shutting the cabin door behind him.

Norita undressed Alyce and slipped her into bed without waking her.

She had just finished doing so when Hignet opened the door softly, as if he knew Alyce would be asleep.

"We've all bin prayin' for you," he whispered with his usual cheery grin.

Norita moved quickly aross the cabin towards him. Outside in the passageway, Hignet asked:

"Wot can I get you, Miss?"

"I am just thirsty," she answered, "and if there is some lime-juice or anything like that, I should be very grateful."

"Chef's waitin' to cook anythin' you want," Hignet said. "There's bin a real 'hullabaloo' here over your disappearance, I can tell you!"

Norita smiled.

"We are safe . . now."

As she spoke she heard the engines start up and knew they were leaving Bahrain.

She could understand that the Marquis wanted to get away and it was something she wanted, too.

Hignet went off to get her what she had asked for and she walked first into her own cabin.

She suddenly felt very limp and once again near to tears.

She knew they were tears of relief and she wished she could just get into bed and cry.

She had the feeling, however, that the Marquis would come to see her to ask exactly what had happened.

Therefore, having washed and tidied herself, she went into the Sitting-Room.

Hignet brought her the lime-juice she had asked for and also a mushroom omelette which the Chef knew she liked.

She ate quickly, more because she thought it would give her strength than because she was actually hungry.

She drank a lot of the lime-juice, saving what was left in the jug in case Alyce should wake in the night and be thirsty.

Then, when Hignet had taken away her dishes, the Marquis came in.

Because she was thinking of him and feeling grateful because he had saved them, she had to resist an impulse to run towards him.

She wanted to hold onto him to make sure he was really there.

Instead she just stood up, her eyes very large in her pale face.

"You are all right?" the Marquis asked.

"Yes . . quite all right . . and Alyce is . . asleep."

"We are leaving this place," he said, "and I can only say how sorry I am that you have been subjected to such an unpleasant and frightening experience."

"I . . I do not want to . . talk about . . it," Norita said. "It is over now . . and you came . . as I felt sure . . you would."

"Why were you so sure?" the Marquis enquired.

"I knew that apart from you wanting to save Alyce, the difficulty of it was a challenge which . . you would be unable to . . resist!"

She spoke just what was in her mind. Then the Marquis said:

"I also wanted to save you!"

There was a note in his voice which made her look at him in surprise.

Then when she met his eyes it was impossible to look away.

Something strange seemed to happen within her breast. She could not explain it, even to herself, and yet she knew it was there, like the twinkling of a star.

Then abruptly the Marquis said:

"Go to bed, Norita! Everything will seem better to-morrow, and I am making plans for the future."

He left the cabin as he spoke and she wondered what he intended to do.

She was also wondering before she fell asleep what he had meant when he said he had found the Perfect Pearl.

129

He was prepared to sell everything he owned if he could possess it.

She puzzled over this for a little while, then as she finally fell asleep she told herself:

"He loves Alyce . . and it is . . something he did . . not do in the . . past."

* * *

The next day Norita felt very tired and weak.

She knew it was only a reaction to having been so frightened, and to be emotionally upset was almost more fatiguing than anything else.

At the same time, it was an effort to play games with Alyce, who, with the elasticity of youth, was in high spirits.

Lady Langley came to the cabin to talk to them both.

When she saw how tired Norita looked, she took Alyce up to the Saloon with her.

"You rest, Miss Combe," she said kindly. "I know what you have been through and it inevitably takes its toll."

Norita knew her advice was good so she lay down on her bed and slept for a little while.

Then Alyce returned. She talked excitedly of the pearls that Lady Bettine and Lady Hermione had found in Bahrain.

It was not very difficult for Norita to understand what had happened.

While the Marquis had been planning with the Resident how he should rescue Alyce and herself, Perry had been instructed to keep the two Beauties amused.

He had therefore taken them to the dealers in the *Suqs*.

They had each found a necklace of large pearls which they expected the Marquis to give them as a present.

"They are not as big as Cleopatra's," Alyce explained to Norita, "but nearly as big as the cherries the Chef gives me!"

"Then the ladies are very lucky," Norita said.

She thought a little wistfully that she would like to have seen the pearls that were to be found in Bahrain a little nearer than she had been able to do.

It was such a relief, however, to be leaving the place that it was impossible to regret anything.

She tried not to remember how frightened she had been in the black tent, nor did she want to think of the dead body of the Arab who spoke English.

Norita thought the *Sea Hawk* was moving more swiftly than she had done previously.

The Marquis did not come to see them, but Alyce went to his Study to say good-night before she went to bed.

"You must thank your Father for being clever enough to rescue us," Norita reminded her.

"I have thanked him already," Alyce replied, "and he said I was to be very good, and not trouble you when you are feeling tired."

Norita felt a warm glow inside her because the Marquis had thought of her.

Now she could think more clearly, she had been half-afraid that he would blame her.

She was responsible for taking Alyce down the cliff to look at the pearls with which the pirates had tempted them.

After she had put the child to bed, and she knew the party would be having dinner in the Saloon, she went out on deck.

They were moving along the coast-line of what she thought was Oman, and she supposed they were nearing the Red Sea *en route* for home.

She could not help regretting that she had seen very little of Arabia or Egypt.

Also, she had little more than glanced at the ports of Europe, where they had stayed only for a very short time on their outward voyage.

"I shall just have to again rely on what I read in books,"

she told herself with a little smile.

Then, as she stood looking up at the stars thinking they were more brilliant than she had ever imagined they would be, somebody joined her at the rail.

She knew it was the Marquis before she turned to look at him, and she felt her heart give a sudden leap.

At the same time, she felt a force surge through her body sweeping away her tiredness so that she was alert and excited.

"I thought I would find you here, looking at the stars," the Marquis said.

"They are so beautiful," Norita answered softly, "and if I never see them again, I feel they will always be in my heart."

"As they will be in mine," the Marquis replied.

She thought it was a strange thing for him to say.

She was thinking how impressive he was in his evening-clothes, when a voice from the other end of the deck shouted:

"We are waiting for you, Selwyn!"

For a moment the Marquis did not move, then he said quietly:

"Good-night, Norita. Take care of yourself."

* * *

The next day Norita awoke to find the yacht was not moving, and realised that they were in harbour.

It was only when she was dressed and had woken Alyce that Hignet came to tell her that they were at Aden.

"I thought we must be," Norita said. "But we got here so quickly!"

"His Lordship's orders," Hignet said, "an' he's already gone ashore to th' British Residency, so look out for changes."

"Changes?" Norita asked.

"His Lordship's bin makin' plans," Hignet explained,

"and I knows only too well what that means!"

Norita felt perturbed.

She did not know why, but somehow she was afraid the Marquis's plans might concern her.

She took Alyce off the yacht, and they walked in the streets around the dock.

She thought that the harbour filled with ships of every description was very interesting.

There were huge *dhows* and several battle-ships, besides a conglomoration of every other sort of sea-going vessel.

Then, as she and Alyce went back on board, she was aware as they passed the Saloon that she could hear the Marquis talking.

The sound of his voice gave her the same feeling she had felt last night when she was looking up at the stars.

She hurried Alyce below, wondering once again what the Marquis was planning.

It was much later in the afternoon that she realised to her astonishment that the Marquis's guests were all leaving the yacht.

For a moment, when she saw their trunks being carried ashore, she could hardly believe it.

An hour passed before Lady Bettine, Lady Hermione and Lord and Lady Langley were all going down the gangway.

There were carriages waiting for them, and Norita wondered what could be happening.

"Why are all Papa's friends going away?" Alyce asked, looking over the railing.

"I have no idea, dearest," Norita replied.

It was then she saw Captain Napier and the Marquis also leaving the *Sea Hawk*.

She was suddenly afraid that she and Alyce were to be the only people left aboard.

The Marquis got into an open carriage which contained Lady Bettine.

As he turned to speak to her, Norita saw him smiling, and it gave her a feeling as if a knife had been thrust into her breast.

'He is going away! He has forgotten me,' she thought.

She knew in that moment that she loved him.

As she took Alyce down for her supper, talked to the child and answered her questions, her whole heart was crying out in protest.

How could she be so foolish as to love a man who was as completely out of reach as the stars in the sky?

It was what he had told her to aim for, but she knew they were like the Perfect Pearl that no one was fortunate enough to possess.

"I love him as Mama loved Papa," she told herself, "but to him I am nothing but his child's Governess."

"You are not listening, Miss Combe," Alyce protested.

"I am sorry, dearest," Norita apologised. "What did you ask me?"

Only when Alyce was in bed and very sleepy did Norita go into her own cabin.

She looked despairingly at the muslin gown with the blue flowers on it that she had just completed.

'There is no point in wearing it now,' she told herself.

Then she was ashamed that she should have thought for one moment that the Marquis would notice what she did or did not wear.

"How can I be so foolish, Papa?" she asked her father, "and why did you not tell me that love was not joy and happiness, but agonising?"

She thought perhaps it might be a long time before she saw the Marquis again.

Perhaps she and Alyce were to be sent home in the *Sea Hawk* while he stayed with Lady Bettine.

It might be a month or more before she even had a chance to see him.

She remembered now how Miss Marsh had said she very

seldom saw the Marquis, and that was what would happen to her.

'I cannot bear it!' she told herself. 'I shall have to find something else to do.'

Then she knew because she loved Alyce that she had no wish to leave the child.

After all, she had been instrumental in making her so very different from how she had been before.

She undressed to have a bath.

Then, defiantly, because she was ashamed of her own thoughts about the Marquis, she put on the kaftan which Alyce had given her.

No one would see her except the Steward, a lad of seventeen, who waited on her while she had supper.

Because she was embarrassed by her own feelings, she felt as if in some way it restored her self-respect.

When she had dressed she looked at herself in the mirror in her cabin. She told herself she looked very different from how she usually did.

The kaftan outlined the slimness of her figure, and because it was exquisitely embroidered it made her feel like an Egyptian Princess.

It flashed through her mind that perhaps one day a man would love her as she wanted to be loved, not because she had what he thought was a beautiful face.

They would feel instinctively drawn to each other so that their hearts and souls were linked by love.

That was what she felt for the Marquis, but he would never feel the same for her.

She turned from the mirror.

He was a star shining thousands of miles away in the brilliance of the sky while she was just a 'Nobody' in the darkness on earth.

There was a knock on the door.

Norita thought it was the Steward telling her supper was ready.

"I am just coming!" she called.

Then she opened the door to find it was Hignet.

"His Lordship's back on board, Miss," he said, "an' asks if you'll dine with him."

"He is back?"

Norita could not help the sudden lilt in her voice, and the feeling as if her whole body was charged with electricity.

He was back! He was here! She knew without asking the question that he was alone.

With an effort she managed to say to Hignet:

"Will you thank His Lordship and say I would be delighted to have dinner with him!"

"I'll tell 'im you'll join him in ten minutes, Miss!" Hignet grinned and was gone.

Norita stood with her fingers clasped together.

He was back and he wanted to see her!

Then she told herself she must be very, very careful. He must not have the slightest inkling of what she was feeling.

He must never guess that she was like all the other women who Mrs. Winter had told her fawned on him because he was so important and so rich.

'If only,' she sighed, 'he was just an ordinary man with very little money!'

It was impossible, as she went up to the Saloon, to stop her heart from turning somersaults, and she found it difficult to breathe evenly.

She had waited exactly ten minutes as Hignet told her to, but the Marquis was already in the Saloon, and looking magnificent.

She thought he looked happy and he smiled at her as he saw what she was wearing.

She walked towards him, and made a little curtsy and he said:

"You look very lovely, and I was sure it would fit you!"

She blushed and wished she had not worn the kaftan,

afraid he would think she had put it on especially for him.

He handed her a glass of champagne saying as he did so:

"We should really have had this last night, but it is easier now we are alone to celebrate what was undoubtedly a triumph of good over evil."

"But .. what has .. happened to .. everybody?" Norita could not help asking.

"I will tell you about that later," the Marquis said. "Now, as I have been busy all day, I am hungry!"

As he spoke the Stewards came in with the dinner.

The meal was delicious, although Norita could only think of how exciting it was to be able to talk once again to the Marquis.

He told her a lot about Arabia without mentioning Bahrain.

He told her how the Pearl had been, and still was, the most important and the most expensive Jewel in the world since the beginning of civilisation.

He told her how Arabia also traded in Frankincense, which Norita found fascinating.

Then he talked to her of Mecca and its great importance to the Muslim world.

It was only when the Stewards came to remove the dishes that they went to the other end of the Saloon, and the Marquis said:

"You were curious to know where everybody had gone, and now I shall tell you my plans."

"I could hardly believe it when I saw their luggage being carried ashore!"

"It is a great relief!" he replied.

She looked at him questioningly and he explained:

"My party had begun to bore me before we reached Bahrain. After what happened to Alyce and you I knew it was impossible to go on listening to their incessant speculation as to what would have happened had they been taken prisoner!"

137

There was a note in his voice that told Norita perceptively how distressed he had been over his daughter's kidnapping.

She could understand his dislike of Lady Bettine and Lady Hermione continually going over it as if they themselves wanted to be part of the drama.

The Marquis, reading her thoughts, said quietly:

"Exactly! That is why I have arranged for them to return to England on a P. & O. Liner which arrived from India this morning."

Norita's eyes widened in surprise and the Marquis went on:

"Fortunately, the Liner was not full, and could accommodate my whole party as far as Marseilles. There they will take the Express train to Calais with my Drawing-Room car attached."

"So . . they have all . . gone!" Norita murmured.

"*All* of them!" the Marquis affirmed. "My friend Perry will look after them and make sure they have every possible comfort."

There was a sarcastic twist to his lips as he added:

"I think Lady Bettine and Lady Hermione will find compensation for any discomfort they suffer in the pearl necklaces I gave them before they left."

"Alyce told me about them" Norita said. "They must have been very . . pleased!"

"They were!"

Unexpectedly the Marquis rose to his feet.

"Last night," he said, "when we were looking at the stars, we were interrupted. Tonight that will not happen"

He put out his hand as he spoke and she took it as he drew her from the chair in which she was sitting.

He did not relinquish it, but took her across the Saloon and out onto the deck.

They walked to the same place on the guard-rail where they had stood the previous night.

Norita suddenly realised that without her being aware of it the *Sea Hawk* had moved from the Quay and was now anchored in the open water at the far end of the bay.

From where they were standing they were looking directly out to sea.

As she expected, the stars were reflected in the water beneath them.

She thought with a smile that the Marquis would tell her how lovely it was.

Then she found he was nearer to her than she expected.

"I brought you here," the Marquis said, "because, Norita, I wanted to tell you that I have found the Perfect Pearl!"

Norita gave a little cry.

"You have? How exciting! I am so glad! You must be very thrilled!"

"Very, very thrilled," he said. "It is something I never expected to find, in fact I thought it never really existed!"

"But you have found it, and I am sure it will make you happy."

"That, of course, depends on you," the Marquis said.

"On me?" Norita asked, thinking she had misunderstood what he had said.

"On you!" the Marquis said firmly.

As he spoke he put his arm around her and, while her head was tilted back looking at him questioningly, his lips came down on hers.

For a moment she was still from sheer surprise.

She had never imagined or thought for one moment that the Marquis might kiss her.

Yet at the touch of his lips she knew that ever since she had known she loved him, it had been a secret dream.

One which she dared not acknowledge to herself.

As he kissed her she felt as if the stars fell down from the skies.

They were in her breast and on her lips and part of the

Marquis so that she merged into him and he made her his.

It was so perfect, so wonderful that she thought that if she died at this moment she would have known an ecstasy and a wonder that was part of God.

The Marquis drew her closer still.

His kiss, which had been very gentle, as if he was afraid to frighten her, became more possessive and more demanding.

Norita was not afraid.

It was something so unbelievably wonderful that she was caught up in a glory and rapture that was beyond thought.

She could only feel and go on feeling that the stars were flickering through her.

That the Marquis was some supernatural being and not an ordinary man.

Then he raised his head and said in a voice she hardly recognised:

"What are you feeling, my Darling?"

"That I love you . . I love you . . and I did not know that . . anything could be so . . marvellous . . so absolutely and completely . . perfect."

"That is what I thought when I first saw you."

Then he was kissing her again until the sea, the stars and the world itself seemed to be whirling dizzily around them.

She heard the Marquis say:

"How can I have been so unbelievably fortunate as to have found what I have always been seeking, even though I was not aware of it?"

"I think . . you mean . . real love," she whispered.

"I mean the love you told me about," the Marquis replied. "The love which I thought existed only in the imaginations of the Poets, and although I would not acknowledge it, in my own heart!"

He pulled her a little closer to him as he said:

"Is that the love you are feeling?"

"I realised . . that I . . loved you, but I never . . thought you would . . love me!"

"I adore you! I worship you! And I cannot tell you how difficult it has been not to tell you so."

He drew in his breath as if he could hardly believe she was real before he said:

"When I learnt that you and Alyce had been taken away by the Arabs I thought I would go mad! I knew then that I loved you as I have never loved anyone in my whole life, and that I could not live without you!"

"How can you . . feel like that about . . me?"

"I can feel that and a great deal more," the Marquis said, "and what I have arranged, my precious little Pearl, is that we shall be married — tomorrow at the British Residency!"

"M . . married?" Norita gasped. 'B . . but . . how can you. . . ?"

"Very easily," the Marquis smiled, "and everything is arranged."

He had fought wildly against his love.

He had tried to ignore the beating of his heart, the vibrations which reached out towards Norita every time he saw her.

But love was too strong for him.

In the darkness of the night he had finally admitted that he loved and needed her.

When daylight came he berated himself for being a fool.

How could he in his exalted position make an unknown girl who was his child's Governess his wife?

"I am mad, crazy," he raged at himself. "I will send her away and never see her again."

Then when she and Alyce were captured he faced the truth — he could not go on living without her.

"But . . how did you . . know that I . . loved you?"

The Marquis smiled.

"Your eyes are very revealing, my Darling, and if you

say you do not love me, I shall kidnap and take you away to some lonely place and keep you there as my prisoner until you have learnt to love me!"

Norita laughed, but it was a choked little sound and there were tears in her eyes as she said:

"But I . . do love . . you! You know I do . . but perhaps it . . would be . . wrong for you to . . marry me."

"How can it be wrong?" the Marquis asked.

He moved his lips over the smoothness of her skin while he waited for her reply, and felt that he was touching the lustre of a pearl.

"You are . . so grand . . so important," Norita replied after a moment, "and I was . . wishing just now that you were an . . ordinary man so I could look after you and . . prevent anyone from . . hurting you."

"That is what you have to do for the rest of your life!" the Marquis said. "But I am not an ordinary man because I love you, and you are not an ordinary woman, because you are perfection itself."

He drew in his breath and added:

"The Pearl for which I am prepared to sell everything I own in order to possess!"

It flashed through his mind as he spoke that that was what he intended to do.

The Social World would certainly be surprised and perhaps hostile at his choice of a bride.

But that was of no importance.

It did not matter to him who Norita was or where she came from.

All he knew was that she was the complement to himself; the woman who was meant for him since the world began.

Perhaps it had taken many lives before he had finally found her.

Norita moved a little closer to him.

"Perhaps if you . . helped me . . I would not make . .

mistakes, as I would not have made them if . . Mama and Papa were alive . . and I would then be the sort of . . wife you want."

"You are exactly the sort of wife I want!" the Marquis said firmly. "I love you, my precious one, not only because you are the most beautiful person I have ever seen."

He kissed her dimple before he continued:

"I also love everything about you: your kindness to my daughter, your sweetness, and the way you never think about yourself."

Norita shyly hid her face against him and he said:

"If I have a lot to give you, you have a great deal more to give me."

"You . . already have . . my love . . my heart and . . I think . . my soul," Norita whispered.

"And tomorrow you will give me your body," the Marquis said, "and that in itself is so beautiful and exquisite that to me it is the greatest Pearl in the world!"

"That is . . what I . . want you to . . think," Norita said. "Oh, teach me . . help me . . show me how to . . love you as you want to be . . loved so that I will . . never disappoint . . you."

The pleading note in her voice, the way she spoke which he knew came from her heart brought the fire into the Marquis's eyes.

He pulled her closer still and kissed her passionately, demandingly, fiercely, until they were both breathless.

Norita was not afraid.

She only felt as if the stars shining within her body were turning to flames, and they were ignited by the fire on the Marquis's lips.

Only when, because she was shy, she again hid her face against him did he say:

"My precious, I must not tire you after all you have been through."

143

"I am not . . tired," Norita protested. "Only very . . very . . excited."

"My sweet, my darling little love!"

His voice was very deep and passionate. Then with an effort he went on:

"Tomorrow, after we are married, the *Sea Hawk* is going to move a little way down the coast to some quiet bay. With only the Arabian sands around us, I will teach you about love."

He kissed her again before he drew her back along the deck and into the Saloon.

In the light he could see that his love had given her a new beauty.

For a moment, they just stood looking at each other.

They were caught up in an indescribable rapture which made it impossible for either of them to move.

All they could feel was the wonder and glory of their love.

At last the Marquis said hoarsely:

"I worship you, my Angel, but because I am thinking of you rather than myself, I am going to send you to bed, but first there are a few things I must know so that our marriage can take place legally in the Church attached to the British Residency."

As he spoke he walked to where there was a writing-desk arranged for the use of his guests.

He found a piece of writing-paper embossed with his crest and sitting down at the table he said:

"First you must tell me your full name."

"Norita Mary Combe."

"And when and where were you born?"

She gave him the details and he wrote it down.

"Now the names of your father and mother."

"My father was . . Lord Wyncombe."

The Marquis looked up at her.

"Lord Wyncombe?"

"Yes. I do not suppose you have . . heard of him because he was . . poor. Only after he died did I . . discover there was . . no money."

"No money?" the Marquis exclaimed.

"That is why I . . went to Miss Marsh who had . . taught me . . to ask for her . . help."

The Marquis drew a deep breath before he said:

"I can hardly believe it!"

"Why? Is there something wrong?"

"No, of course not," he replied, "but you are in fact The Honourable Norita Combe!"

"Miss Marsh told me I was not to use . . my title because it might . . cause . . difficulties with . . the staff," Norita explained. "She said they would feel . . embarrassed if they knew I . . was a . . Lady."

The Marquis put down his pen.

He had intended to marry Norita if she was only a poor Governess as he had thought her to be.

But his friends would be very curious about her, and sooner or later somebody would have mentioned the fact that she had been employed by him.

That her father was a Nobleman would make all the difference.

Not to him, but to the Social World in which, as his wife, Norita would inevitably belong.

He stared down at the paper on which he had written Norita's name and that of her father.

He told himself he was even luckier than he had thought himself to be.

Now there would be no difficulties for her family or his friends.

He had sent his party away simply because he wished to marry Norita without them gossiping about it and perhaps sneering at him for doing so.

He had also wanted to prepare Norita and give her confidence before he introduced her to his relatives.

Now there was no necessity for that or for any secrecy about their marriage.

He, knew, however, that he intended to have a very long honeymoon before he took Norita back to England.

He had not yet told her what he had arranged with the British Resident and his wife.

They had asked the Marquis if he would take their daughter, who was the same age as Alyce, and her Nurse as far as Marseilles.

Then his little girl was returning to England to be with her grandmother.

It fitted in with the Marquis's plans because the Nurse would look after Alyce.

The British Resident was quite prepared for his daughter to take a long time on the voyage.

The doctors had advised him not to let her stay in the heat of Aden during the summer months which was why she was going back to England.

Everything had fallen so neatly into place that the Marquis could hardly believe it.

He saw everything passing through his mind like a kaleidoscope: the happiness he would find with Norita, first in the quiet peace of Arabia.

The joy they would have together when they left the children with the Nurse in Alexandria, so that he could show Norita the Pyramids in Cairo.

After that, they would leisurely make their way homeward, stopping at Naples, Venice and eventually at Marseilles.

He would be able to buy her the clothes with which he wanted to frame her beauty.

He knew to do so would thrill, excite and delight them both.

All in all he thought it was the most ambitious plan he had ever made because it was a plan for happiness.

Then he realised that Norita was looking anxiously at

him, with a touch of fear in her eyes.

"Why are . . you so . . silent?" she asked. "Have I said . . something wrong?"

She went a little nearer to him, saying with a sob in her voice:

"You have not . . changed your . . mind? Perhaps you do not wish to . . marry me . . after all?"

"My darling, my foolish, adorable little Pearl," the Marquis said. "I was in fact sending up a prayer of thankfulness that I have found you, and that we will be so happy together!"

He rose and put his arms round her to hold her close against him.

"Tomorrow," he said, "I shall vow to love you for the rest of my life. That is what will happen. It is something which will never change or alter, and our love will grow, year by year."

"That is . . what I want to . . believe."

The Marquis looked down at Norita and said very gently:

"The Perfect Pearl! I have one for you which is the largest to be found in the whole of Bahrain! And while that will be yours, you will be mine! You are my 'Perfect Pearl', my darling, and completely and absolutely beyond price."

"You are . . sure of . . that?"

"As sure as the stars will be there tomorrow," he said, "so that we can look at them together, and know that for us, at any rate, they are within reach."

Norita gave a little cry.

Then he was kissing her. Kissing her wildly, passionately, possessively, as if he was afraid he might lose her and was determined to make her his.

She could feel the fire burning from his lips to hers, and the flames from it were flickering through her body.

She knew it was all part of the real love they had for each other.

147

The love that was part of the Divine Spirit of God, yet also human and compassionate.

"I love . . you! I . . love you!" she wanted to say, but there was no need for words.

They had both in their own way found the 'Perfect Pearl' which all people seek.

It is in fact the love which comes from God, and is God, now, tomorrow, and on to the end of the world.